Fast as the Wind

A Novel

Nat Gould

Fast as the Wind: A Novel

The present edition is a reproduction of previous publication of this classic work. Minor typographical errors may have been corrected without note; however, for an authentic reading experience the spelling, punctuation, and capitalization have been retained from the original text.

ISBN: 978-1-63637-467-3

CONTENTS

CONTENTS

CHAPTER I

THE BOOM OF A GUN

A small but splendidly built yacht steamed slowly into Torbay, passed Brixham and Paignton, and came to anchor in the outer harbor at Torquay. It was a glorious spring morning, early, and the sun shone on the water with a myriad of dancing reflections; it bathed in light the beautiful town, the scores of villas nestling on the heights surrounding it, the palms on the terrace walk, on the mass of greenery clothing foot to summit, on the inner harbor, and on the rocky coast stretching out towards Anstey's Cove and Babbacombe Beach. It was a magnificent sight, the arts of man and nature mingled together, for once harmonizing, for Torquay has not been spoilt by builders, at least as seen from the bay. Behind, Brixham way, the red sails of the fishing boats flapped lazily in an idle breeze. Four men-of-war lay still in the bay, guardians of the peace, comforting, reassuring, a hint of what lay behind. How peaceful these monsters of the deep looked. Slumbering surely were they. What was that? A puff of white smoke, then a solemn sound, which sped across the bay, and echoed over the hills. One of the monsters had spoken, just to show it was wide awake.

It had a curious effect on the man leaning over the side of the Sea-mew, the yacht that had just come to anchor. It startled him from his reverie, from his contemplation of all that was so beautiful around him.

For a moment he looked across at the warships, and saw the smoke drifting away, then he turned and looked over the town and its heights, and his thoughts went far and landed on Dartmoor.

Another gun boomed out. This time it seemed more natural. Again the echo ran over the hills, and again he turned and looked towards that vast moor which lay behind.

"Supposing it were true," he muttered. "Would to God it were, and that he were safe on board my yacht. All for a woman, and such a woman!"

He clenched his fist and struck the rail.

Picton Woodridge, owner of the Sea-mew, was a man of about thirty, tall, good looking, genial, popular, but lonely, if a popular man can be described as lonely, and there are such men. He was rich, a sportsman. His stable at Haverton contained good horses: a Derby winner in prospect, one of the best stayers in England, and

1

above all Tearaway, a black filly, three years old, described by her trainer, Brant Blackett, as "a beauty, a real gem, and fast as the wind."

He ought to have been a happy man. To all outward appearances he was, but behind a smiling face there is sometimes a heavy heart. It was not exactly so in his case, yet there was something of it. There was one black shadow cast over his gilded path, and the echo of the gun from the man-of-war had deepened it.

"Why the deuce did I come here?" he muttered. "Why did I promise Dick I'd ride for him at Torquay races?"

He sighed; he knew why he had promised Dick Langford to ride for him; he would do a good deal more than this for Dick, for the sake of his sister Rita. He had no other companion on the yacht than Ben Bruce, captain of the Sea-mew, who stood towards him in the light of his best friend.

Ben Bruce was a character in his way. He had been in the Navy, on the same ship with Picton's father, and Admiral Woodridge and the young officer had esteem and affection for each other. Lieutenant Bruce often came to Haverton in the Admiral's time and was always a welcome guest. He had known Picton from a boy, and shared the Admiral's fondness for the somewhat lonely child, whose mother died at his birth, and whose elder brother was generally away from home, training for the Army. Bruce remembered the elder boy, Hector, but had not seen so much of him, or become so attached to him as to Picton. Hector was of a different disposition, hasty, headstrong, willful, and yet the brothers were much attached, and when at home together, were seldom apart. There were ten years between them; consequently Hector regarded himself in the light of a protector to Picton.

The Admiral loved them and endeavored to treat them equally in his affection, but it was not difficult to see the younger had the stronger hold over him. Hector saw it and smiled. He was not at all jealous; he felt if it came to choosing, and one of them had to be relied upon, his father would select him. And such would probably have been the case had occasion occurred, but it did not, and everything went on the even tenor of its way until the fatal day when a terrible thing happened and Hector became, so Picton was positively certain, the victim of a woman's wiles. What this happening was we shall learn. Sufficient to say, it caused the Admiral to retire. He never got over the shock, and died soon after he left the Navy. The bulk of his fortune was left to Picton, who was determined, when the time came, to surrender to Hector his proper share. Captain Ben Bruce left the service soon after the Admiral he had loved and served. He was, so to speak, a poor man, and when he

2

came to Haverton, to his old chief's funeral, Picton begged him to stay with him for a few months to relieve his loneliness. This he readily consented to do. The months extended, and Picton would not let him go; he relied on the stronger man, who had carved his way upward by his own exertions. Ben Bruce protested, all to no purpose.

"I can't do without you," said Picton. "You were my father's friend, he had every confidence in you; you are one of the executors, you are the proper man to remain here and run the show."

Ben Bruce laughed.

"Run the show!" he said. "Not much chance of that even if I wished it. You've a good head on your shoulders, and one quite capable of managing your affairs. If I stay, mind I say if, it will not be on that account."

"It doesn't matter to me on what account you stay so long as you consent to remain," said Picton. "There's so much to do here; I am short of a companion—you know I don't take to everyone. There's another thing—although you're a sailor you are fond of horses, and a good rider, and I say, Ben, I've a proposition to make."

Again Ben Bruce laughed.

"You've got a fresh proposition almost every week, and it's nearly always something in my favor."

"This will be to your liking, as well as, if you think so, in your favor."

"What is it?"

"Take charge of the Haverton horses—be my manager."

"What about Blackett?"

"He'll not mind; in fact he'll like it. I put it to him; he seemed rather enamored of the prospect of being closely connected with Captain Bruce, the friend of his adored Admiral. There wasn't a man living Blackett loved more than my father; I think it was the combination of the sea and the stable appealed to him. Blackett always had an idea, so he told me, until he became acquainted with the Admiral, that sailors were duffers where horses were concerned. 'But I soon found out the difference,' he said; 'the Admiral knew pretty near as much about a horse as I did. Of course I taught him a thing or two, but he was a good judge, he knew the points of a horse pretty near as well as he did the parts of a battleship.' That's Blackett's opinion, and he has an idea Captain Bruce has leanings in the same direction as the Admiral, so you can't raise any objections on that score."

It did not take much persuasion to induce Captain Bruce to consent, and he became manager of Haverton Stables and, as a natural consequence, remained with Picton Woodridge.

At the same time Picton said to him, with a serious face:

3

"There's something else, far more important than anything I have mentioned. You've to help me to clear Hector; you believe him innocent, don't you, Ben, you can't do otherwise?"

Ben Bruce was silent for a moment—Picton watched him anxiously—then said, "Yes, I am sure he is innocent. He couldn't have done that, not to secure any woman for himself; but it's a mystery, Picton, a grave mystery, and it will take a far cleverer man than myself to unravel it. I'll help you, I'll stick at nothing to help you and Hector."

"Thanks, old friend, thanks a thousand times. With your help there is no telling what may be accomplished. There must be some way out of it; such a terrible injustice cannot be allowed to go on for ever," said Picton.

And so Captain Ben, as he was called, became the constant friend and companion of Picton Woodridge. When the Sea-mew was purchased it was Captain Ben who clinched the deal, and was appointed "skipper."

"So I'm your stud manager and captain of your yacht, that's a queer combination," said Ben.

"And you're as good in one capacity as the other," said Picton.

"I think I'm safer on deck than on a horse," said Ben.

It was Captain Ben Bruce who came quietly along the deck of the Sea-mew and looked at Picton Woodridge as he gazed over Torquay bay. A kindly look was in his eyes, which were always bright and merry, for he was a cheerful man, not given to look on the dark side of things. His affection for Picton was that of a father for a son, in addition to being a companion and a friend. He noticed the sad far-away look on Picton's face, and wondered what it was that caused the shadow on this beautiful April morning.

"I'll leave him to his meditations," he thought; "he'll be down for breakfast, and I'll ask him then."

He was about to turn away when Picton looked round and said with a smile: "Something told me you were there."

"Telepathy," said Ben.

"Sympathy," said Picton. "Do you know what I was thinking about?"

"No; I saw you were pensive. I'd have asked you at breakfast, you looked so serious."

"I was serious."

"What caused the passing cloud on such a glorious morning?" asked Ben.

Picton took him by the arm, his grip tightened; with the other hand he pointed to the battleship.

"The boom of a gun," he said; and Ben Bruce understood.

4

CHAPTER II

STORY OF AN ESCAPE

ROW me to the Sea-mew," said Dick Langford, and old Brackish touched his cap and replied, "Yes, sir; she's a beauty, she is. Hear the news, sir?"

"No; anything startling?"

"Nothin' out o' the common, at least not in these parts, but it's summat different to most."

"You're always long-winded, Brackish—Yorkshireman, I suppose," said Dick impatiently.

Brackish was a Yorkshire boatman, hailing from Scarborough; he came to Torquay because his mother, nearly ninety, could not stand the cold blasts of the North East coast, and the old salt had a heart. "Brack" had a rough red face, eyebrows lapped over a pair of blue eyes; his throat and chest were always bared, tanned the color of leather; black hair covered his chest; his hands were hard, a deeper brown than his chest, the hands of a son of toil, and a boatman. Brack had been popular at Scarborough; he was well known in Torbay as a brave hardy seaman, whom no weather daunted. At first he had joined the Brixham fishing fleet, but soon tired of it, and when he saved enough money he bought a couple of boats, and made a decent living in Torquay harbor.

Brack was fond of gossip, and on this particular morning he was eager for a talk; it was his intention to have it out with Dick before he put foot in the boat, so he stood looking at the young man, barring his entrance to the craft he was eager to put his foot in. The old boatman was a sturdy figure in his rough seaman's clothes as he eyed Dick Langford, and, although impatient, Dick could not help smiling at him. He liked Brack, and the sailor returned the feeling.

"Let me get in and you can tell me about the news as we row to the yacht," said Dick.

"All right, sir; no hurry, you're here early. It's Mr. Woodridge's yacht, ain't it?"

"Of course it is; you know the Sea-mew as well as I do."

"Nice gentleman, Mr. Woodridge," said Brack.

"If you don't let me get into the boat I'll take another," said Dick.

Brack grinned.

5

"You'll not be doin' that, I'm thinking, after all I've done for yer."

"What have you done?" asked Dick surprised.

Brack looked indignant.

"Yer don't recollect? Well I'm blessed! Fancy forgettin' things like that!"

"Out with it," said Dick.

"I give yer the winner of the Leger three year runnin', and it's forgotten. Lor' bless us, what memories young gents has!" growled Brack.

Dick laughed heartily as he said: "So you did, old man. You're a real good tipster for the Yorkshire race."

"So I ought'er be. Don't I hail from there? I can always scent a Leger winner, smell 'em like I can the salt from the sea, comes natural somehow," said Brack, as he moved away and allowed Dick to step in. He pulled with long steady strokes and was soon out of the inner harbor, making for the yacht.

"By jove, this is a lovely morning!" said Dick, looking at the glorious hills he knew so well.

"Nowt like Yorkshire," growled Brack.

Dick laughed as he said: "You're a lucky man to be at Torquay, all the same; much warmer, fine climate."

"Hot as——," said Brack with a grunt.

"You haven't told me your news," said Dick.

"It'll keep," said Brack.

"Bet you a shilling you let it out before you reach the Sea-mew," said Dick.

"I don't bet," said Brack.

"You mean you dare not in this case, or you would lose."

"Very like I should, because I see yer burstin' to hear it, and I wouldn't like to disappoint yer," said Brack, as he ceased rowing and leaned on his oars.

"Tired?" said Dick.

"With that bit of a pull," said Brack, disgusted; "I should think not!"

"Then what are you resting for?"

"I baint restin', I'm easin' my oars."

"Oh, that's it: the oars are tired," said Dick.

"No more tired than I am, but when I gives 'em a spell for a few minutes they seems to work better," said Brack. "What's more, I talks better when I leans on 'em, sort o' gives me composure, and time to think; I'm a beggar to think."

Dick was amused; he wanted to reach the Sea-mew, but on

6

this sunny morning it was good to sit in the boat on the blue smooth water and listen to old Brack for a few minutes.

"You must have done a lot of thinking in your time," said Dick, falling into his humor.

"I'm thinking now," said Brack.

"What about?"

"That poor devil who escaped from Dartmoor five days ago."

Dick smiled.

"Is that your news?"

"Yes."

"There have been several escapes lately."

"But they've all been caught in no time; this chap ain't, and by gum, lad, if he come'd my way I'd help him out. I don't believe they'll get him; at least I hopes not."

"They'll have him right enough," said Dick. "A convict at large is a danger to all on the moor."

"This one ain't," said Brack. "'Sides, he may be innocent."

"Innocent men don't get into Princetown," said Dick.

"That's just where yer wrong," said Brack. "I've a brother in there now, and he's innocent, I'll swear it."

Dick maintained a diplomatic silence.

"Of course you'll not believe it, but it'll come out some day. He was on a man-o-warsman, and they lagged him for knocking a petty officer overboard; the chap was drowned, but Bill swore he never had a hand in it, and I believes him. At the trial it came out Bill had a down on the man; and no wonder—he was a brute, and a good riddance."

"Do you know who knocked him over?"

"No, but it's my firm belief Bill does, and that he's sufferin' for another, won't give him away."

Dick smiled.

"You don't know Bill; I does," said Brack emphatically.

"But what about this man who escaped? Why do you think he'll get away?"

"'Cause he's a good plucked 'un, a fighter, a brave man," said Brack.

"In what way?"

"They put bloodhounds on his track. One brute got away, they didn't find him for three days, when they did——," Brack hesitated; he wished to rouse his listener's attention. He succeeded.

"Go on," said Dick eagerly.

"The trackers found the hound dead, and alongside him was a suit of convict clothes—nice well marked suits, ain't they; you can't mistake 'em," said Brack.

7

"You don't mean to say the fellow killed the hound, and left his clothes beside it!" exclaimed Dick.

"That's just what I have said, mister. Clever, weren't it? When the other hound found his mate, he found the clothes, and he lost the scent."

"How?"

"'Cause the man must have fled stark naked, and the hound only had the scent of his clothes; must have been that, 'cause he couldn't follow him. He'll get off right enough—you see if he don't. I wish Bill could do the same."

"How did he kill the hound?" asked Dick. "And where did you hear all this?"

"Strangled it. He's a good 'un he is; I'd like to have seen it. As for how I come to know by it, one of the men from the prison was here. He questioned me," said Brack with a grin. "Asked me if I'd seen a man like the one he gave a description of."

"What did you say?" asked Dick.

"Kept him talking for half an hour or more, gave 'im heaps of information. I filled him up, never you fear."

"But you didn't see the man?" said Dick.

"Lor' no! Wish I had, and that he was stowed away somewhere. I told the fellow I'd seen just such a man as he described, with his hands bound up in bandages, and a cloth round his neck. Said he'd a suit of old sailor's togs on, and that he went out in a boat with a lot of rowdy fellers to a 'tramp' in the Bay, and he didn't come back," chuckled Brack.

"And what was the result of your false information?" asked Dick.

"I'll tell you what the result will be. It will put 'em off the scent; they'll think he's gone off on the 'tramp' to London, and they'll give him a rest on the moor for a bit," said Brack.

"You think the man is still on the moor?"

"'Course; where else should he be?"

"Then he's sure to be caught."

"Wait a bit—a man who can tackle a bloodhound and choke the life out of him is pretty determined," said Brack.

Dick acknowledged as much and said the circumstances were out of the common. He was interested in the old sailor's tale. He did not know whether to admire what Brack had done or to condemn it; he put himself in his place, wondering how he would have acted under similar circumstances.

Brack watched him, a peculiar smile on his face.

"Goin' to give me away?" he asked.

8

Dick laughed as he answered: "I was thinking whether you were right or wrong."

"Guessed as much. I was right to give such a man another chance. He's no coward, not he, and guilty men are all cowards," said Brack.

"Who is the man?"

"Don't know; he wouldn't tell me, but he said he was a lifer. He didn't seem very keen about his capture."

"You mean he seemed glad the man had escaped?" said Dick, surprised.

"I guessed as much from his face," said Brack, "and I reckon there's worse judges than me of human nature—that's what makes me think he's innocent—like Bill."

"It's all very interesting, but pull to the Sea-mew," said Dick.

"About time," said Brack, as he started rowing again. They were soon alongside the yacht.

Picton had just come on deck again from the saloon. He hailed Dick cheerfully.

"Well, early bird, what's brought you here at this time?" he said, smiling.

"Wished to welcome you, most mighty rider of winners," laughed Dick as he got out of the boat and stood on the steps of the gangway. "Here you are, Brack, and thanks for your story; it was thrilling."

Brack touched his cap as he said: "And it's true, and there's heaps of things thrilling that ain't true," and he pulled away.

"Brack been spinning yarns?" said Picton, who knew the old man.

"A real shocker this time."

"What about?"

"A fellow escaped from Dartmoor the other day. It's worth hearing; I'll tell you all about it later on," said Dick.

Picton Woodridge staggered backwards. At first Dick thought he was about to fall. He looked at him in astonishment.

"What's the matter, Pic?" he asked.

"Curious fit of faintness came over me; I'm all right now," said Picton, but Dick thought he didn't look it.

9

CHAPTER III

THE MAN ON THE ROAD

DICK Langford told Brack's story to Picton Woodridge and Captain Ben. Both listened attentively: it was immensely interesting to them. From time to time Ben looked at his friend to see how he took it. Dick, absorbed in his tale, did not notice the look of strained attention on their faces. They were silent when he finished.

"Not bad for Brack, eh?" said Dick.

The simple question made them start.

"You fellows seem all nerves this morning," said Dick. "When I told Pic on deck, he staggered; I thought he was going to faint. You're not afraid the fellow will board the yacht, are you?"

Ben laughed as he said: "No, I don't think we're afraid, not of one man, even if he be an escaped convict."

"You'll want all your nerve to-morrow," said Dick to Picton. "There's three of my horses to ride, and two of 'em are brutes."

"Thanks," said Picton, smiling; "a pleasant prospect. Worth coming all these miles for, isn't it, Ben?"

"Depends upon what Langford calls a brute," replied Ben.

"Pitcher's not so bad; he's what I call a humorous horse, full of pranks and no vice about him. He's number one. Now we come to the first brute, Planet, a gelding with a temper; as likely as not he'll try and pitch you into the crowd."

"Then he ought to have been named Pitcher," said Picton.

"We don't all get our right names, I mean names that fit; we're saddled with 'em by unthinking parents. Sis has a maid, Evangeline Mamie; now that's what I call a big handicap for the girl," said Dick.

They laughed, and Picton asked him to pass on to number two brute.

"The Rascal," said Dick; "he's a terror. He's lamed a couple of my chaps, and Pete's right when you're in the saddle, but it's a deuce of a job to get there. He rises on his hind legs, and conducts an imaginary band with his fore legs, but he's got a rare turn of speed, and he ought to win the West of England Handicap Steeplechase to-morrow, and the Torbay and South Devon Steeplechase the next day."

"Then you expect to bring off the double with him?" said Picton.

10

"Yes, and if you do not, Sis says she'll never speak to you again."

"Then I'll do it if I die in the attempt," said Picton.

"Don't be heroic, no one wants you to die. You can kill The Rascal if you like, but promise me to come off unscathed," said Dick, laughing.

"I'll try," said Picton.

"Pitcher ought to win the Maiden Hurdle Race, and Planet the St. Marychurch Hurdle Race. Now you have a nice little program mapped out for you, and I fancy you'll win the four events. If you do, it will be a day for rejoicing at Torwood, and the wearer of the pink jacket will be an honored guest if he cares to desert the Sea-mew for my humble abode."

"Dick, you're incorrigible," said Picton, laughing. "You really expect to win four races?"

"I do; Gordon won the lot at a meeting not far away on one occasion."

"That's quite possible—he's a good rider."

"So are you."

"He is," said Ben; "few better."

"What are you doing to-day?" asked Dick.

"Nothing in particular; basking in the sunshine in your glorious bay."

"Then you like Torquay?" said Dick.

"Who could help liking it? And what a county lies behind it! I envy you the Devonshire lanes, Dick."

"Then come and live among them. I can pick you an ideal spot, and it shall be well within your means, Mr. Millionaire."

Picton laughed.

"No millions here—a few thousands," he said; "just sufficient to keep my head above water."

"And the Sea-mew afloat," said Dick.

"I'll manage that," said Ben.

"Will you come ashore and have a look at Pitcher and the two brutes?" said Dick.

"What do you say, Ben? Shall we?" asked Picton.

Ben knew he wished to go—Rita was at Torwood—it was not the horses so much, although they were an attraction.

"Yes," said Ben promptly, and the matter was settled.

They went ashore. Dick Langford's dog-cart was at the Queen's and thither they adjourned. In a quarter of an hour they were going at an easy pace to Torwood, which lay about midway between Torquay and Newton Abbot.

How fresh everything looked! The trees were just budding,

tingeing the almost bare branches with tips of green. The air was cool and soft; there were no motors about—only an odd one or two, the tourist season had not commenced—but there would be plenty of people at the races on the following days.

"Wonder what that fellow's up to!" exclaimed Dick, as he saw a man push through the hedge and disappear down the hill and across the meadow.

"Probably belongs to the place," said Picton.

"Then what the deuce did he get through the hedge for? Why didn't he go to the gate?" said Dick.

"Short cut, perhaps," said Picton.

"Wonder if he's that chap from Dartmoor?" laughed Dick, and he felt Picton start.

"The man's got on your nerves," he said. "I'll say no more about him."

Picton was looking at him as he went rapidly across the meadow; something about the figure appeared familiar, so did the long stride; he wondered if Ben noticed it, but the Captain was otherwise occupied. The incident was forgotten, and when they came in sight of Torwood, Picton became animated. He saw a figure on the lawn, and knew who it was. She recognized them and waved her handkerchief. This met with a quick response.

Torwood was a typical Devonshire home, not large, but a commodious, comfortable, well-appointed house, standing on the hillside; trees at the back, a terrace, then a level stretch of lawn, then a sweep down to the road; a small lodge and gate at the drive entrance; a steep incline to the house. On the right were the stables, half a dozen loose boxes, and a three-stall building. Dick Langford was far from being a rich man, but he was happy and contented, with his sister. He was a partner in a firm of auctioneers at Newton Abbot, and was accounted a ready salesman; there was always laughter in front when he wielded the hammer; quick at repartee, there were many people prompt to draw him out, but he got his prices, and that paid the firm and the customers.

Rita Langford was like her brother, of a bright and cheerful disposition, was popular in the neighborhood, and Torwood was a favorite house.

"So glad to see you, Mr. Woodridge, and you too, Captain Bruce. When did you arrive in the bay?"

"In the morning, yesterday; it was beautiful. How grand the country looks, and Torwood even prettier than ever!" said Picton.

"I induced him to leave his floating palace, and visit our humble abode, by asking him to inspect the horses he is to ride," said Dick with a wink at Ben.

12

"That is so, but there was a far greater inducement," said Picton, looking at Rita.

"Must I take that to mean me?" she said, laughing.

"Please," said Picton, thinking how charming she was.

They had a quiet luncheon, then went to the stables. Dick engaged no regular trainer, but he had a man named Arnold Brent, who was a first-rate hand with horses, and at the same time an expert gardener; the combination was fortunate for the owner of Torwood. The horses were trained in the neighborhood, where Dick had the privilege of using some good galloping land, with natural fences—an up and down country, but excellent for the purpose. He had two lads who rode most of the work; sometimes he had a mount, and occasionally Brent. Altogether they did very well, and the Torwood horses generally secured a win or two at the local meetings. Dick Langford's favorite battle-grounds were Torquay and Newton Abbot. At the show at the latter place he often took prizes for dogs, poultry and garden produce; the money generally went into Brent's pocket. Brent knew both Picton and the Captain, and admired the former because he knew he was a first-class gentleman rider, although he had not seen him in the saddle. It was Brent who suggested to his master that Mr. Woodridge should ride at the local meeting for them.

"Not a big enough thing for him," said Dick doubtfully. "He rides at some of the swell meetings."

"You try him, sir," said Brent, adding, as he caught sight of Rita, "I'll bet he accepts."

"I hear a terrible account of these horses I am to ride," said Picton, smiling.

Brent smiled.

"I expect Mr. Langford's been pulling your leg, sir," he said.

"Isn't The Rascal a brute, isn't Planet another; and Pitcher was described as harmless, I think?" said Picton.

"The Rascal's all right if you humor him," said Brent. "He's bitten a lad, and crushed another against the wall, but he's not half a bad sort, and he'll win the double easily enough in your hands, sir."

"If I can mount him," laughed Picton.

"I'll see to that; he'll stand steady enough with me at his head. That's him—the chestnut with the white face."

Picton looked the horse over.

"Bring him out," he said, and The Rascal was led out of his box. As Picton went up to him he laid back his ears, and showed the whites of his eyes; it was a false alarm, he let him pat his neck and pass his hand over him.

"I like him," said Picton; "he looks a good sort."

13

"He is, sir," said Brent.

"Your favorite?" laughed Picton.

"Yes, sir."

Planet and Pitcher were both browns, handy sorts, and Picton thought it highly probable the three would win the races selected for them. He expressed this opinion, at which Dick and his sister were delighted.

"It is very good of you to come and ride for my brother," she said to him.

"It is always a pleasure to me to do anything to please you and Dick," he replied.

They chatted for some time; then she said: "I had an adventure not long before you arrived."

"Your country has always been full of adventures," he said, smiling.

"And adventurers, but the man who came here to-day was not an adventurer, poor fellow," she said.

He looked at her quickly and she went on.

"I was at the bottom of the garden, near that thick-set hedge, when I heard some one groan. It startled me; some tramp, I thought, and went to the gate. I saw a man sitting by the roadside. He looked up when he saw me, and I shall never forget the suffering in his face, the hunted look in it. I shivered, but I was quite sure he was harmless. I beckoned him; he came, turning his head from time to time in a frightened manner. He said he had tramped many miles, that he was hungry, footsore, weary to death. I took him to the back of the house, gave him something to eat, and offered him money. He refused the money at first, but I insisted and he took it. I gave him one of Dick's old top coats; when he put it on he seemed a different man. I hunted out a pair of old boots—he was very grateful for them. I am sure he was a gentleman; he spoke like one, he expressed himself as such when he left, there was a natural pride about him. He walked in the direction of Torquay; I wonder if you met him on the road."

Picton Woodridge greatly astonished her by asking her the following questions:

"Have you told your brother about this?"

"No."

"Did any one see him?"

"I don't think so. I am almost sure they did not."

"Will you do me a favor?"

"Willingly."

"Then do not mention this to a soul," said Picton earnestly.

14

CHAPTER IV

THE WOMAN AT THE TABLE

SHE promised readily, not asking questions, for which he was grateful. She knew there was something she could not penetrate, some mystery; her curiosity was aroused but she restrained it.

"Thank you," he said. "I have good reasons for asking you to remain silent; some day I will tell you them, whether my conjectures prove right or wrong."

"I shall not ask your confidence," she said.

"I will give it to you. I would give it to you now if I thought it would be of any use."

"I am sure you would."

"Rita——"

"Hallo, where are you, Picton?" shouted Dick.

"Here!" he called. "On the seat near the hedge."

"Oh, down there. Is Rita with you?"

"Yes."

"Sorry I shouted; hope I didn't disturb you," sang out Dick.

"Not in the least," said Picton; "we were just coming up."

"I wonder what he was going to tell me when he said 'Rita,'" she thought as they walked up the hilly garden path.

Picton said he would rather return to the yacht for the night; he loved being on the water, it always had a soothing effect and he was not a good sleeper.

"I must be in tip-top condition for to-morrow—so much depends upon it," he said, smiling.

Rita thought a good deal about her conversation with him when he left, tried to puzzle out the mystery, but failed.

"I'll wait until he tells me," she said. "I wish Dick hadn't shouted when he said 'Rita'; it interrupted a pleasant sentence. I wonder how it would have finished?" and she smiled quietly to herself.

Dick drove them to Torquay, then returned home. Brack rowed them out to the Sea-mew. He was loquacious as usual.

"Nice night, gents," he said.

"Beautiful, Brack. Isn't it rather dark though?" said Ben.

Picton seemed moody.

"Yes, there's no moon to speak of; it's darker than I've known it at this time o' year."

15

The old fellow chatted until they came alongside.

Picton paid him and said good-night. Brack thanked him and said: "Goin' to ride any winners to-morrow, sir?"

This roused him and he told Brack the names of the horses and the races they were going for.

"You back The Rascal for the double if you can find any one to lay it to you," said Picton.

"We've a bookie among us," said Brack. "He's a young 'un and as good a sailor as the best of us, but he's artful, very artful, and he's had many a bob out'er me, and the rest. I'd like to take him down, and I will. The Rascal for the double, you said?"

"Yes, and here's half a sovereign to put on him," said Picton.

Brack gave an audible chuckle as he said: "Lor' love us, that'll just about bust him if it comes off."

They laughed as he rowed away, whistling softly to himself.

"I'll turn in early," said Picton.

"The best thing you can do," said the Captain. "You seem a bit out of sorts to-day."

"I am; I can't get the sound of the gun out of my ears."

Ben looked at him sympathetically.

"I knew what you meant, felt what you felt, when you spoke about it," he said.

"Strange some one should have escaped from Dartmoor a day or two before," said Picton.

"Escapes are often occurring," said Ben.

"What did you think about that man on the road, who pushed through the hedge to avoid us?" asked Picton.

"Didn't give it more than a passing thought," said Ben.

"What was the passing thought?"

"I said to myself, 'I wonder if that's the man who escaped?'"

"Good-night," said Picton; "I'll turn in."

"Good-night," said Ben, as he sat on a deck chair.

"He's in a curious mood to-night," he thought. "I'm sorry for him. We ought not to have come here, it brings up painful recollections, the vicinity of Dartmoor; and yet it has its compensations—there's Miss Langford, lovely girl, and as nice as she looks. I hope he'll win to-morrow, it will cheer him up."

Ben's mind went back to the time when Picton and Hector were lads together, and the Admiral was alive. His heart was sore for Hector, although he was half inclined to believe him guilty, but tried to convince himself to the contrary by expressing his firm belief in his innocence, in order to be of the same mind as Picton.

One thing Captain Ben had long determined upon: if ever he got a chance, he would help Hector, no matter at what risk or cost.

He was a man who had run into many dangers, not useless dangers, necessary perils, with his eyes open, knowing the consequences of failure, therefore he was a brave man. Blindfolded, impetuous, blundering rushes against great odds excite the admiration of the crowd, but it is the Captain Bens who are to be relied upon in times of emergency.

The air became cooler. Ben rose from his chair and went to his cabin; looking into Picton's as he passed, he was glad to see him asleep.

The Sea-mew swung round with the tide, quietly, without a sound; it was very still and calm; she looked like a dull white bird on the water. So thought a man who crept stealthily along the wall toward the inner harbor.

"I wish I were on her and out at sea," he muttered. He could just discern her outline, the white hull and the lights.

He heard footsteps, a measured beat, a policeman, he knew by the tread. He put his hand on the wall to steady himself, shivered, then groaned. There was no getting out of it, he must face the man, and it was late. He staggered forward with a drunken reel, but not too unsteady on his legs. He lurched, just avoiding the constable, who merely said: "Now, my man, get off home, and mind you keep quiet."

"All right, sir, I'm a'goin'," was the reply.

The constable moved on, blissfully ignorant that he had probably missed a chance of promotion. The man walked past the pier, past the Torbay Hotel, where there were lights in one of the rooms on the ground floor, evidently a late supper party, at least so thought the man outside. Do what he would, he could not resist the temptation to cross the road and see what was going on. There was a chink in the blind. At first he saw little, his eyes were curiously dim and heavy from lack of sleep, gradually the mist in them lifted. He saw four people seated at a table, brilliantly lighted, a dainty supper spread. It was long since he had seen such things, but he had been used to them. Naturally, being hungry, he looked at the well-laden table; then his eyes went to the people sitting there, two men and two women. He saw the men first, then one woman, then the other woman, and his eyes started, his hands clenched, his face went livid, his teeth met with a snap; for a moment he stood thus, regarding the woman with a fixed stare of horror. She was a beautiful woman, voluptuous, with a luring face, and eyes which knew every language in every tongue of unspoken love. She was smiling into the eyes of the man at her side as she toyed with a dainty morsel on a silver dessert fork. She was dressed with excellent taste, expensively, not lavishly. She was a woman who

17

knew overdressing spells disaster. Her white teeth gleamed as she smiled; the man at her side was lost in admiration—it was not difficult to see that.

The man looking outside raised his clenched fists and said: "Is there no God, no justice anywhere?"

As he spoke the woman dropped her fork and started, a shiver passed over her. The man at her side hastily got up, brought her a wrap and placed it on her shoulders. The man outside saw the fork fall, he saw the wrap, and he muttered again: "There is a God, there is justice; her conscience imprisons her as surely as——"

"Move on there! What are you lurking about here for?"

"All right, goin' 'ome, just met yer brother along there."

"He's not my brother," said the constable gruffly.

"Thought yer were all brothers, members of the same cloth, anyhow yer all good sorts. Good-night."

"Be off home," said the constable, as he went on his way; and a second man lost a chance of promotion that night.

"I must not run any more risks," thought the man, "but I'm glad I crossed the road and looked in at that window. She suffers, she could not have heard my voice, perhaps an internal justice carried it to her and my words were whispered in her ears—such things have been known. There she sits, feasting, surrounded by every comfort, but she's not happy, she never will be, such women never are. God, to think what I have gone through for her, what I have suffered! I have lived in hell, in purgatory, and I ought to be on my way to heavenly peace. God, give me a chance; I am an innocent man and You know it."

"Hallo, mate, where goin'? Yer a late bird," said Brack, as he knocked against the man walking in a curiously wild way in the middle of the road.

"Goin' 'ome," said the man.

"That'll not get over me; yer puttin' it on. I'm fra Yorkshire, and a bit too cute for that."

"What d'yer mean?"

"That I've heard gents speak in my time, and I reckon you're one."

The man started; at first he was inclined to bolt; then as the light of a lamp shone on Brack's face he saw it was honest, kindly, full of charity, and through it he knew there was a big heart inside the rough body.

"You are right," he said. "I was a gentleman, I hope I am one still, although I have lived such a life that the wonder is I am not a beast."

Brack looked hard at him; from his face his gaze wandered

18

over his body, then he looked at his hands; one was bound up, the other had marks on it, deep marks, like the marks of teeth. Brack made up his mind.

"Don't move," he said, "when I tell you something. I'm a man, not a fiend, and I've an innocent brother over there," and he jerked his hand in the direction of the moor far away. "Maybe you've seen him."

The man gasped—this old sailor knew! Should he—no, the face was honest, he would trust him.

"Perhaps I have," he said.

"Are you the man that throttled that bloodhound?"

"Why do you ask?"

"Because if you are I'd like to clasp yer hand and say I think yer brave."

The man held out his bandaged hand; the old sailor took it in his big, horny palm tenderly, pressing it gently.

"The other one," he said.

The man held out his other hand.

"I'm glad I've held 'em both, the hands that strangled that cursed hound. Come along with me. I'll see yer safe, never fear. There's not a man jack of 'em in Torquay or Princetown, or anywhere, would ever suspect old Brack of harboring a—gentleman."

Without a word the man went with him. As he walked at the honest Brack's side he thought: "My prayer has been answered."

CHAPTER V

PICTON'S WINNING MOUNTS

IT was Easter Monday, and a holiday crowd gathered on the slopes of Petitor racecourse at St. Mary Church. More than usual interest was shown in the meeting owing to the presence of Picton Woodridge, whose fame as a gentleman rider was well-known. Dick Langford was popular and the success of the pink jacket eagerly anticipated.

Petitor is not an ideal course; it is on the slope of a hill, and a queer country to get over, but some interesting sport is seen and the local people take a pride in it; as a golf links it is admirable.

Picton had not seen the course before, at least only from the road, and as he looked at it he smiled.

"I may lose my way," he said to Rita; "go the wrong course."

"You will find it easy enough, and you are not likely to make mistakes. Look," and she pointed out the track to him, and the various obstacles.

There were bookmakers there—where are they not when races are on, no matter how small the fields, or the crowd?

Picton wore the pink jacket, ready to ride Pitcher in the Maiden Hurdle Race, the opening event. There were only three runners, and yet the books accepted six to four on Dick's horse; there was a strong run on Frisco; and Fraud was nibbled at.

"Come along," said Dick; "time to mount."

"Good luck!" said Rita with a smile. "You'll find Pitcher easy to ride. I've been on him several times."

"He'll find me rather a different burden," said Picton.

The three runners came out, and Picton received a hearty welcome, which he acknowledged.

"Sits his horse well," said one.

"A good rider, anybody can see that."

"Here, I'll take seven to four and it's picking up money!" shouted a bookmaker; and so thought the backers as they hurried up with their money, and Pitcher quickly became a two to one on chance.

The distance was two miles. Picton indulged Frisco with the lead until half a mile from home, when he sent Pitcher forward, had a slight tussle with Frisco, then forged ahead and landed the odds by ten lengths amidst great cheering.

"Win number one," said Dick triumphantly; "when the meeting is over they'll bar you from riding here again."

Rita was delighted, her face all smiles; she was proud of the good-looking man who had carried her brother's colors to victory.

Picton, as he walked about with Rita, Dick, Captain Ben and a host of friends, was the cynosure of all eyes; but he was accustomed to being stared at.

"Now comes the tug-of-war," said Dick. "There's The Rascal. See how he's lashing out, scattering the crowd. I believe he's in a nasty temper, confound him."

There were five runners in the Steeplechase, and although The Rascal had Picton up, the favorite was Anstey, who had Hordern in the saddle. The Tor, Moorland, and Stream, were the other runners, but wagering was confined to the favorite and The Rascal.

Picton walked up to his mount; The Rascal switched round, despite Brent's efforts, and refused to be mounted. His rider watched him with an amused smile; Dick and his sister looked anxious, while a crowd gathered round at a respectful distance.

Picton bided his time, then, when The Rascal had his attention attracted by Brent, slipped up to him, took the reins and swung into the saddle, and before the astonished horse recovered from his surprise he had him well under control. The spectators cheered; it was a clever piece of work, deserving of recognition. Once mounted, The Rascal seemed tractable enough; but Picton knew the horse was not in the best temper, and required humoring.

"You've not got a very nice mount," said Hordern as they rode together.

"I'm told he's queer-tempered," said Picton; and as he looked at Anstey he thought: "Your mount will take a bit of beating."

They were soon on their journey. At first The Rascal made a deliberate attempt to bolt; he discovered he had a rider who refused to put up with his inclinations in this direction. Finding bolting stopped, he tried to swerve at the first fence; this object was also frustrated and he received a few stinging cuts from the whip, wielded by a strong arm. These vagaries allowed Anstey and the others to forge ahead, and The Rascal was in the rear.

Dick looked glum, but Brent said: "There's plenty of time. He's a rare turn of speed—and a grand rider up."

At the end of the first mile The Rascal was still last. He began to improve his position; quickly passed Stream, and Moorland, then the Tor; but Anstey was a dozen lengths ahead, fencing well. Two more obstacles then the run home. Picton rode The Rascal hard to find if he would respond to his call. Whatever else he was, the horse was game, he did not flinch, and Picton was surprised how easily he

21

went ahead. Anstey blundered at the next fence, Hordern making a fine recovery; this cost the favorite several lengths. At the last fence The Rascal was only three or four lengths behind. Anstey cleared it well, The Rascal struck it, stumbled, threw Picton on his neck, struggled up again; and Picton was back in the saddle and riding hard before the crowd realized what had happened. Then a great cheer broke out, for a splendid bit of jockeyship.

"Not one man in a hundred could have done that," said Brent enthusiastically.

Hordern thought he had the race won. The Rascal on his knees, with Picton on his neck, was good enough for him. He took a pull at Anstey; he intended winning the double, and did not wish to press him too hard. It was a blunder; he found it out when he heard the cheering and cries of, "Well done, Picton!" "Rascal's catching him!" The stumble seemed to put new life into The Rascal, for once again he showed what a rare turn of speed he possessed.

Picton rode his best.

"Rita expects me to win—I will," he thought; and something told The Rascal it would be bad for him if he failed to do his best.

Two hundred yards from the winning post Anstey led, but it had taken Hordern a few moments to get him going again when he realized the situation. It was dangerous to play these games with Picton. The Rascal came along, moving splendidly; he gained on Anstey, drew level, held him, then got his head in front. Hordern rode well, but he had met his match. The Rascal drew ahead and won by a length amidst tremendous cheering—Picton Woodridge was the hero of the day. Rita was proud of him and told him so at Torwood the same night. The Rascal had been backed to win the double with every man who had a book on the races, so next day the excitement rose to fever heat when the Torbay Steeplechase came on for decision.

The Rascal was in the best of tempers, he actually allowed Picton to stroke his face, pat his neck, and pay him sundry attentions; Rita gave him lumps of sugar, and said he was the dearest and best of Rascals.

"You will win the double," she said to Picton. "I am sure of it."

"And I'll try to win a far richer prize before long," he said, looking at her in a way that caused the red blood to mount to her cheeks.

Anstey ran again, but the main opposition was expected to come from Sandy, a Newton Abbot horse. Dick's horse had to give him a stone, which was a tall order, but Brent said he could do it, unless Sandy had improved out of all knowledge.

"I'd take The Rascal to the front this time," said Brent to

22

Picton; "he's in a good temper and when that is the case he likes to make the pace, and he jumps freer."

"If he'll do it, I'll let him," said Picton. "Will he stay there? Remember he's giving lumps of weight away."

"He can do it," was the confident reply.

Six runners went out, a field above the average at Petitor.

Most people thought some of the runners would have been better out of it, they would only be in the way, a danger to the others at the fences; a blunderer is often a veritable death trap.

It astonished Leek, who was on Sandy, to see Picton take The Rascal to the front. He smiled as he thought, "He's making a mistake this time."

Evidently the others thought the same, for they patiently waited for the leader to come back to them.

Arnold Brent smiled.

"I gave him good advice. They're doing exactly what I thought they would, waiting. Let 'em wait."

The distance was two miles and a half. The Rascal held a big lead at the end of a mile and a half. Leek on Sandy thought it was about time he came back to him, but The Rascal showed no sign of this; on the contrary, he gained ground. To go after him was the best thing and Leek tried. Much to his astonishment, he discovered the pace was much faster than he thought; Sandy made very little headway. At first Picton's policy of making the running was considered a mistaken one; this opinion changed as the race progressed; and when they saw Leek hard at work on Sandy in second place and making hardly any headway, The Rascal's numerous backers were jubilant. The cheering commenced, it became deafening as Picton drew near to the winning post. It was an extraordinary race. The Rascal, the top weight, made all the running and won by twenty lengths; more than that, he was not in the least distressed.

Picton was congratulated on all sides. Turning to Dick and Rita he said: "He's one of the best horses I have ever ridden over fences; there's a National in him."

Dick shook his head.

"You're too enthusiastic. Wait until you've cooled down," he said.

"I shall not alter my opinion," said Picton. "Where's Planet?"

"Over there," said Dick, and they walked across.

The next race was the Marychurch Hurdle Plate, and Picton rode Planet. The race needs little description; there were three runners, and Dick's horse won comfortably.

At Torwood that evening there were great rejoicings; but as

Picton wished to sleep on the Sea-mew he and Ben were driven to Torquay.

Before he left, Picton said to Rita: "Next time I am here I have a very important question to ask you."

"Have you?" she said. "I wonder what it is."

"Cannot you guess?"

"I'll try," she answered, smiling happily.

"It's too important to put in a hurry," laughed Picton, "and I haven't the courage to do it now."

"Not after four victories," she answered, laughing.

He shook his head, as he got up beside her brother in the trap.

"If you won't sell The Rascal, send him to Haverton," said Picton as they bade Dick good-night.

"All right, I will, and you can do what you like with him," said Dick cheerily.

"Brack's not here; that's strange. We shall have to get some one else," said Ben.

They hired a younger man. He happened to be the boatmen's bookie.

"Where's Brack?" asked Ben.

"He backed the double with me for half a sov.," said the man. "He's about broke me, sir, but I don't begrudge it him; he's a real good sort. I expect he's celebrating it in town."

Brack was not celebrating it; he was biding his time, and opportunity.

CHAPTER VI

IN BRACK'S COTTAGE

BRACK'S was a humble abode not far from the inner harbor. He lived there with his mother. The old woman idolized him; he was a very good son. She attended to their small wants and kept the house scrupulously clean.

"I've brought a mate, mother," said Brack as he entered with his companion.

"He's welcome, my boy." She always called him her boy, and somehow it did not sound strange.

"Come in, don't be afraid," said Brack.

The man stepped into the small room, looking round suspiciously. Why had Brack brought him here, had he any particular reasons for doing so, reasons that would benefit himself?

Brack gathered something of what was passing in his mind and whispered, "You'll be quite safe here, sit down."

They had a fish supper; to the stranger it was the most wonderful meal he had partaken of for some years. He ate greedily, he could not help it, but Brack, watching him, knew he was a well-bred man.

The old lady asked no questions, she never questioned what her son did; she bade them good-night and went to her room. It was then Brack learned something of the man he had brought to his home; and the tale harrowed his feelings, froze the marrow in his bones, horrified him; he shuddered as he imagined what this highly cultured man must have suffered.

They talked until the small hours of the morning, Brack considering what he should do, how to get his companion away from Torquay?

Suddenly he said, "Do yer mind telling me yer name? I'd like to know it in case I hear of yer in the world sometimes. You'll be far away from here, but I'd like to have something to remember yer by and I reckon yer name's the best thing."

The man was startled; again the suspicious look came into his eyes. Would it ever be entirely absent, that haunted gaze; it was pitiable.

"I don't want it if you don't care to give it to me."

"I beg your pardon. You deserve my entire confidence. You

25

are running grave risk for my sake, an unknown man, a stranger, worse—an escaped prisoner from Dartmoor."

"Never mind the risk; we'll not trouble about that," said Brack.

"Do you know what the consequences would be if it were known you had hidden me?"

"I don't know and I don't care," said Brack.

"Think of your mother."

Brack laughed as he said: "She'll glory in what I've done when I tell her; she's Bill out there."

"I forgot; that makes all the difference. And he's innocent."

"Like you."

"How do you know I am innocent?"

"Yer face tells me. I'd trust a man like you anywhere and anyhow."

"If ever I come into my own again, if ever my innocence is proved, I'll see to you and your mother for life, and I'll promise to do all I can for Bill, your brother."

Brack's face glowed.

"Damn me but you're a man!" he said and seized his hand. "I forgot, I'm a fool," he added, as the man winced. The pain from Brack's honest grip was intense.

"I will tell you my name. You may have heard it before—we receive news sometimes—my brother is a famous rider. You are a bit of a sportsman?"

"I am," said Brack. "I've had a tip for the races here, for the double, and I've got ten bob to put on; the gentleman who's goin' to ride gave it me. He says to me as I left the yacht—I'd rowed him out there—he says, 'Here, Brack, there's half a sov. for you. Back The Rascal for the double.' And I mean to."

"The Rascal?"

"That's the name of the horse—funny, isn't it?"

"Who was the gentleman?"

"The owner of the Sea-mew, the yacht lying at anchor in the bay."

"The yacht with such beautiful lines, painted white? I just saw her as I came along by the wall before I met you, my good friend."

"That's her. She's not big but she's a gem. She's been here several times."

"And who is the owner?"

"The same as rides Mr. Langford's horses at the races."

"But you have not told me who he is."

"Ain't I? No more I have! It's Mr. Picton Woodridge."

The man stared at Brack; he seemed on the point of falling off his chair.

26

"Picton Woodridge," he said in a hoarse voice.

"Yes; have you met him in days gone by?" asked Brack.

"He is my younger brother," said the man. "I am Hector Woodridge."

It was Brack's turn to stare now. This man he had brought to his home Picton Woodridge's brother? Was it possible? This was indeed a strange chance! He peered into his companion's face, trying to trace a resemblance, and found one.

"Yes," he said, "you're like him, or you were once."

Hector Woodridge sighed.

"Once," he said; "it all seems such a long while ago."

"I remember, I recollect now," said Brack. "I wonder it did not strike me afore. Yer a Yorkshire family. I know, at Haverton. I was a boatman at Scarborough when it happened. I always said you were innocent; I call to mind the trial well. Yer Mr. Hector Woodridge, thank God for that; I see a way out of it all. You must bide here and I'll pick the night when I can get you away."

"Get me away!" exclaimed Hector. "How, where shall I go?"

"Leave that to me. There's a man on the watch here. His name's Carl Hackler. He's from Dartmoor, and he's prowling around here on the lookout—has been for a week or more."

"I don't remember his name," said Hector.

"Likely enough not; there's plenty of 'em there as you'd never see, but he's seen you, and he'd recognize you. I've fooled him once and I think he knows it; I'll have a stiff job to do it again; but I will do it, and you'll get clear away."

"What is your plan?"

Brack hesitated; he wondered if Hector Woodridge would care to go on board the Sea-mew, whether he would be afraid to implicate his brother. He decided it would be better for his purpose not to say what his plan was until he had his man safe in his boat on the way to the yacht.

"I'll tell you that when the time's ripe. You'd best turn in and have some sleep; you look as though you could do with it."

"I can. Where shall I go?"

"In there," said Brack, pointing to a small room.

"It is your room."

"Never mind me. Go in and rest."

Hector was dead beat. He opened the door, he was so exhausted he fell fast asleep before he had time to undress.

Brack sat ruminating until an early hour. This discovery that his guest was Hector Woodridge stunned him, he could not comprehend it. He recollected all about the celebrated trial which resulted in Hector Woodridge being condemned to death for the

27

murder of the husband of the woman he had become entangled with. All Yorkshire signed the petition for a reprieve and the sentence was commuted to penal servitude for life. He remembered how the shock killed Admiral Woodridge, Hector's father.

Brack went to the old black horse-hair sofa and lay down. He was soon asleep, dreaming in a few minutes, strange dreams in which convicts, Dartmoor, the Sea-mew, The Rascal, Carl Hackler, and divers and other persons and places were mixed up in the most extraordinary manner.

A knocking at the door roused Brack.

Sitting up, he rubbed his eyes, yawned, struggled to his feet. He had his sailor clothes on.

Another knock.

"Comin'. Don't be in such a hurry. Leave the milk can, yer fool."

Another knock.

"Must be deaf. Drat the lad, what's he wakin' an honest man up at this hour for?"

He went to the door, unlocked it, pulled back the bolt, opened it, and found Carl Hackler standing before him.

As Brack said afterward: "I wish I could 'ave pushed him into the harbor, me a'top of him."

"'Morning, Brack. I want a boat; can you come quick?" said Carl.

Brack's relief was so great that he gave a loud, startling laugh.

"What the deuce is the matter with you? Have you suddenly gone mad?"

"Sane as you are, Mister Hackler," said Brack. "Maybe a bit saner at times."

"I believe you fooled me about that man being rowed out to the tramp. Anyhow the tramp's here, put back for something I suppose, and I'm going to board her before she leaves again, and question the skipper. I particularly want you to row me out because I mean to tell him who gave me the information while you are alongside," said Hackler.

"Now I call that nice of you," said Brack. "Here I gives you the best tip I can and you want to get me into trouble if it's correct. I did my best for yer, Mr. Hackler, on my honor."

"Will you row me out?" said Hackler impatiently.

"What's it worth?"

"Five shillings."

"I'll be with you in a minute," said Brack. "I'll just tell mother."

28

"Let her know her little boy is going out in good company," said Hackler.

"I'll tell her who I'm goin' with, then she can judge for herself, whether the company's good or bad," replied Brack.

Hackler laughed as he said: "You're a smart chap, Brack."

"Am I? Then perhaps you can find me a job out your way."

"Better where you are," said Hackler, with what sounded very much like a sigh.

Brack went into his mother's room. She was awake.

"What is it, lad?" she asked.

"Hush, mother! I'm goin' out with Hackler in my boat. He's the man from Dartmoor, on the lookout for the escaped prisoner. I'm rowin' him out to the tramp; she's put back again."

She smiled; she knew all about it.

"Tell him not to stir out of that room until I comes home. He'll sleep a good while. He must not come out, not even in here—you understand, mother?"

"Yes, but who is he?"

"He's the man Hackler's after; the man who strangled the bloodhound. He knows our Bill. He's a gentleman; he'll do what he can for him when he's proved his innocence. He is——"

"Come on, Brack; don't be all day," called Hackler.

"I'll see to him, lad, never fear; he's safe with me," said his mother.

"Comin'," said Brack as he went out and joined him.

CHAPTER VII

A CRITICAL MOMENT

BRACK, as I remarked before, you are a smart fellow. Were you putting me off the scent when you said the man I am looking for went off in the tramp?" said Hackler.

"I never said he were the man; I said there were a man went off with the boat's crew to the tramp."

"I gave a description of him."

"It seemed like him to me," said Brack.

They reached the harbor; Brack pulled in his boat; Hackler stepped in and was rowed toward the tramp. The dirty looking steamer was farther out than anticipated, and Brack took his time; his practiced eyes discerned something invisible to Hackler.

"Steam up," said Carl.

"Most likely she'll be going in an hour or two."

"I wonder what she put back for?" said Hackler half to himself.

"Short o' coal," grinned Brack.

"Shut up and don't be a fool," growled Carl.

Brack could see the steamer as he looked sideways over his shoulder. A humorous smile stole over his face.

"She's movin'," he thought.

There was a stir at the stern of the tramp, the screw revolved, she was steaming away, and Carl Hackler was too late. When he recognized this he lost his temper; he had taken his journey for nothing. Catching sight of Brack's face, he fancied he detected laughter there; this did not improve matters.

"Confound you, I believe you knew she was going!" he said angrily.

"Not until the screw turned," said Brack.

Hackler stood up in the boat and waved; some one on the tramp answered the signal but she continued on her way.

"D——n the fellow, why doesn't he stop!" raged Carl.

"Looks suspicious, but he doesn't know who you are. If he did he'd be sure to slow down," said Brack.

Carl turned round quickly; he had an idea he was being chaffed and didn't like it. He stumbled, barked his leg on the seat, fell forward, and sprawled in the bottom of the boat. He did not know a sudden spurt by Brack caused this.

30

He floundered about, smothered his rage as best he could, then ordered Brack to row him back.

"Hope yer not hurt," said Brack sympathetically.

No answer was vouchsafed to this polite inquiry.

"Looks as though he might be aboard that tramp," said Brack. "They got off pretty sudden; perhaps you were recognized."

"Who'd have recognized me?" asked Carl.

"Him as yer looking for."

Carl laughed.

"Not likely; I don't think he ever saw me."

"But you've seen him?"

"Scores of times."

"You'd know him again?"

"Of course; he's easy to recognize. But they've probably got him by now."

"Poor chap."

"Call him that, do you? You'd not do it if you knew what he was there for."

"Tell me."

"He shot a man whose wife he had been carrying on with. It was a brutal, cold-blooded murder. The husband found them together; they were fairly trapped, so the fellow shot him."

"Funny he should carry a revolver about with him," said Brack.

"It wasn't his revolver, it was the husband's; that's why he was reprieved. It was argued that the weapon was in the room, that on the spur of the moment he picked it up and shot him."

"Oh," said Brack meditatively. "I suppose it never occurred to you, or the larned judge, or the blessed jury, that some one else might have shot him."

Carl laughed.

"Who else could have shot him?"

"It's not for me to say; I'm not clever enough. She might 'a' done it."

"Who?"

"The wife."

"What nonsense! He confessed he did it."

"Eh!" exclaimed Brack.

"I say he confessed he fired the shot."

"And he says he's innocent," said Brack.

Carl stared at him.

"Says he's innocent!" he exclaimed. "How do you know?"

Brack saw his mistake and quickly covered it.

31

"I lived in Yorkshire at the time. I know all about the trial; I read it."

"Oh," said Carl. "If you read it you know more about it than I do."

"Very likely," said Brack as the boat went alongside the steps. Carl landed; he gave Brack half a crown.

"Five bob," said Brack.

"But you didn't go to the tramp."

"I couldn't; she was away."

"Then you can't claim the lot," said Carl, who was annoyed at missing the steamer.

"I suppose not exactly," drawled Brack, "but betwixt gents, I should say it holds good."

Despite his annoyance, Carl could not help laughing.

"I suppose you must have it," he said, and handed him another half-crown.

"Goin' home to-day?" asked Brack.

"Home!"

"To Dartmoor."

"That's not my home."

"It's where yer located, at any rate."

"I don't know. There's no trace of the man. It's queer where he's got to; I fancy he's dead—fallen down a mine, or been starved out."

"That's about it," said Brack. "Fancy looking for him round here! Seems a bit soft to me."

"You take a lot of interest in this man," said Carl eying him closely.

"No more than I do in any man who makes a fight for liberty."

"Would you let 'em all loose on Dartmoor?" sneered Carl.

"I'd chance it if there were any innocent men among 'em."

"There are none."

"There's one I know of."

"Who?"

"My brother Bill."

Carl laughed as he said: "Your brother Bill was lucky not to be hanged," and walked away.

Brack scowled after him and muttered: "And you'll be lucky not to be drowned if yer not careful."

When Brack arrived home he told Hector Woodridge what happened.

"By gad, he gave me a shock when he came to the door this morning," said Brack. "You must wait for to-night; I'll come and fetch you if the coast is clear. You'll have to trust me, leave it all to me."

"I will," said Hector. "I can do nothing for myself."

"You can do a lot. If there's danger keep cool and don't betray any alarm—face it out."

"I place myself entirely in your hands," said Hector.

There was no chance that night. Brack stayed about the harbor until ten o'clock. Just as he thought the opportunity favorable Carl Hackler turned up, and Brack made for home, thinking he had not been seen. He was mistaken.

"Something mysterious about the old fellow lately," thought Carl. "He can't know anything; it's absurd, of course; but I'll swear he put me off the scent about that tramp. Confound him, he's a shrewd 'un, he is. It's my belief No. 832 is in Torquay somewhere. There'll be a shindy if he gets away, because he's got a lot of rich relations I believe; somebody's sure to say it's a put up job. There wasn't any put up business about strangling that dog; I can't help admiring the fellow for that. He bore a good name in the prison too."

"No go to-night," said Brack as he came in, "but I've got a bit of news."

"What is it?" asked Hector.

"I've won the first part of my bet with The Rascal."

Hector could not help smiling; it seemed a curious piece of news under the circumstances. He said: "I hope you'll win the double."

"It'll mean a fiver to me," said Brack, "and that's a lot to a poor man."

"You shall have a pocket full of fivers when I prove my innocence," said Hector.

"I'd not take 'em," said Brack. "I'd be satisfied to know I'd done you a good turn, that I would," and he meant it.

Next evening Brack was very well pleased with himself when The Rascal won the double. He proceeded to draw his money and enlighten the youthful bookie on the follies of gambling; he also exhibited some liberality in the matter of drinks to several mates.

He saw nothing of Carl Hackler, although he walked about the streets and loitered near the water.

"I'll try it to-night," he thought. "The races are over and maybe the Sea-mew will sail before morning. There's no telling, and it's the best chance there is; it can't be missed; it's too good, even if we run some risk. If I only knew where that Dartmoor chap was. I'd give half my winnings to know—I'd give the whole blessed lot to get him safe on that yacht."

Brack went home full of his plan, and how best to manage it without exciting suspicion.

It was after ten o'clock when he slipped out of the house. Hector Woodridge followed at some distance, keeping him in sight.

"He's going to the harbor," thought Hector. "What will he do there?"

Brack looked round in every direction as he went down the steps and hauled in his boat. It was no unusual thing for a boat to go out at night to a man-o'-war, or to some craft lying in the bay, but he was not fond of such work and knew if any of his mates saw him it would attract notice. Looking up, he saw Hector leaning over, and beckoned him to come down.

"Once we're out of the inner harbor there'll not be much danger," said Brack. "Chuck that waterproof over yer shoulders; it'll keep yer warm and it looks seaman-like. Now we're ready."

"Hallo, Brack!"

He looked up and saw Carl Hackler on the steps peering at the man in the boat. Brack had wonderful control. It was a matter of more than life or death to Hector Woodridge; if Hackler got him he would be sent back to his living tomb, for such it was to him.

"Oh, it's you!" said Brack with as much contempt as he could master. "And pray what are you doing here? Want another trip in the bay? If you do, jump in and I'll take you. I've got the mate of the London Belle here; he's a bit overseas and I'm taking him out. Ain't that right, Harry?"

"That's the job, Brack, that's it," hiccoughed Hector, who guessed the danger was great.

"I've half a mind to come," said Carl, not quite satisfied, but utterly deceived by Brack's cool manner.

"You'll have ter make up the other half quick," said Brack.

"I'll leave you to it. Mind your mate doesn't fall overboard," said Carl.

"I'll see to that," said Brack.

A hoot came across the bay, a peculiar sound. Brack knew it; it came from the Sea-mew.

He sat down and pulled his best. Would he reach her in time?

Carl Hackler watched the boat until it was out of sight.

The hoot came again.

"What's that steamer sounding?" he asked a sailor close to him.

"The Sea-mew; she'll be leaving to-night, I reckon."

Carl started. Was it possible? No, of course not. What a fool he was; and yet, Brack was rowing as though his life depended on it.

34

"Better make sure," he muttered, and turning to the boatman said: "Will you row me out to the London Belle?"

"Yes, sir, how much?"

"Half a sovereign," said Carl.

Another hoot came across the bay from the Sea-mew.

CHAPTER VIII

ON BOARD THE "SEA-MEW"

I wonder if the beggar'll follow us," gasped Brack, between his spurts; "seemed mor'n half inclined to it—cuss him for his meddling!"

"Where are you going?" asked Hector.

"To the Sea-mew."

Hector started—his brother's yacht. He must not go there. What would be the consequences if he were taken on her, found concealed? Picton would be compromised, in grave danger, probably of imprisonment.

"I cannot let you go there," said Hector; "it is impossible."

"Just you sit still. You're a'goin' there whether you like it or not," said Brack doggedly.

"I will not place my brother in a false position."

"What'd you do if he were in your place and came to the yacht as you're doin'?"

Hector made no answer; he knew he would take the risk.

"There y'ar," said Brack triumphantly; "I knew it. You'd take him aboard and gie him a hearty welcome."

"Put back; I won't go," said Hector.

"Put back, eh, and land yer right in his arms. Not me, not for Brack, oh dear, no; you just sit still, will yer?"

Brack had a peculiar habit of saying "you" and "yer," and sundry other words, changing them as the mood took him.

"Now I'd not be at all surprised if he'd hired a boat and was on his way to the London Belle, just to scent out things; he's a human bloodhound, d——n him, that's what he is."

"If he goes to the London Belle he'll find out we have not been there and he will guess we have come to the Sea-mew," said Hector. "I cannot risk it, Brack."

"Leave him to me. We'll reach the Sea-mew long afore he can get to the Belle. That's her out there, right beyond the yacht. I'll put you aboard and row round to her like h——, and I'll meet him comin' to her if so be he's set out; I'll see he doesn't board her if I have to run him down."

Brack was pulling with all his might; the boat seemed to skim through the still water of the bay like a skiff; they were nearing the Sea-mew.

36

Captain Ben Bruce was on deck, looking over the side. They were about to leave the harbor; Picton was anxious to get away. He was in the cabin. Ben left him reading; probably he had fallen asleep after the excitement of the day.

He heard the sound of oars, and in another minute or two saw the boat shooting toward the yacht.

"Who's this coming here?" he wondered.

He made no sound, merely watched, wondering what would happen.

Brack did not see him as he came alongside; the gangway steps were up; how was he to get Hector aboard?

"Is that you, Brack?" said Ben.

"It's me, sir. Let down the steps quick. I've something to say to you, something that won't keep."

"As particular as all that?"

"Yes, a matter of life or death," said Brack.

"We're just about to leave the harbor."

"For God's sake, let down the steps!" said Brack.

Hector did not move or speak; his nerves were strung to the highest pitch, he quivered all over.

Captain Ben called a hand and they opened the gangway and lowered the steps.

"Now's yer time—go up quick!" said Brack.

"Who's that?" asked Ben, as Hector rose up.

"He's comin' aboard; he's a friend of Mr. Woodridge's."

"Who is he?"

"He'll tell you when he's aboard," said Brack.

"That won't do for me," said Ben.

"Don't yer trust me?" asked Brack.

"Yes."

"Then, for God's sake, let him aboard or you'll regret it for the rest of your days."

"Come up," said Ben, thinking it passing strange the man did not give his name.

Hector hesitated; Brack urged him on.

"Go, go! Think what I've got to do—row round by the Belle in case he's after us."

Hector hesitated no longer; he could not leave Brack in the lurch, and if Hackler found out they had not rowed to the Belle there would be trouble. He got out of the boat; no sooner was he on the steps than Brack pushed off and shot away. Ben called after him but he did not stop; he was making for the London Belle as fast as he could row.

"Who are you?" again asked Ben as he came on deck.

37

Hector trembled with excitement; he was unstrung, he had suffered much; the chase over the moor, the battle with the hound, the naked flight, hunger, exposure, the fear of being taken, the suspense of the past few days brought on a burning fever. He tried to speak but could not; his tongue clove to the roof of his mouth; his lips were parched; he held out his hands in a helpless fashion; he staggered, reeled across the deck. Ben gazed at him in wonder. He could not make it out. There was something very mysterious; Brack must have known what he was doing.

Hector groped along the deck like a man walking unsteadily in his sleep; he mumbled to himself, looked from side to side furtively, began to run, stopped, knelt down, put his face close to the deck in a listening attitude. Ben watched him, followed him. Was this a madman Brack had put on board?

Presently Hector came across a coil of rope. He seized it with both hands and wrestled with it in his fierce grasp.

"Strangling some one," thought Ben.

"You beast, you're dead, ha, ha, ha, I've done for you!" and the weird laugh sounded doubly strange on the water.

Hector rose and pulled off his coat, then stripped off his shirt.

"I must stop this," said Ben. He stepped forward and was about to take him by the arm, when Hector whipped round and flung himself on him.

"You'll never take me alive, never, I'll die first! Kill me if you like—I'll never go back!" hissed Hector, as he clenched Ben by the throat. It was an easy matter for the Captain to hold him off at arm's length, a strong man against a weak, and as he did so he saw into his face by the light of the lamp behind him.

Something in the face roused memories in Ben. He looked long and earnestly. The fever-stricken man returned his gaze; the poor tired brain had a glimmering of reason again. Thus they stood, gazing, forging the past, piecing links together in a chain of recollection.

"Ben, Ben, don't you know me?"

It was a bitter, heartbroken cry, a wail of anguish, and it struck Ben like a knife, it seemed to cut through him. As Hector's cry ceased he fell forward into Ben's arms. Like a flood the incidents of the past few days rushed into Ben's mind. The boom of the gun, the escape of the convict, Brack's story, the strangling of the bloodhound, the man on the road to Torwood.

"Great heaven, it's Hector!" said Ben. "Poor fellow! My God, what a wreck!"

Then his thoughts flew to Picton. It would never do to let him know to-night; he must be prepared for the shock. Where to conceal

38

Hector? For the present, at any rate, he would put him in his cabin. The hands on board—could they be trusted? Some story would have to be concocted. There was a man near and Ben called him.

"Help me to carry him into my cabin," said Ben.

The sailor obeyed without a word. He was an elderly man; he had served with Captain Bruce on the Tiger.

"Say nothing of this until I give you permission," said Ben.

"Right, sir," said Abe Glovey.

"Abe, you are much attached to Woodridge and myself?"

"I am, sir."

"Can you persuade every man on board to keep this man's presence here a secret? It's very important."

"It shall be done, sir. They are all good men and true."

"Mr. Woodridge will reward them handsomely if nothing transpires ashore."

Hector lay on Captain Ben's bunk, and they stood looking at him.

Ben took a sudden resolution.

"Abe, I will confide in you, tell you a secret, which if disclosed means ruin to us all, and a living death to him."

"I think I understand, sir."

"You guess who he is?"

"I know, sir. A terrible change has come over him, and no wonder, but I can recognize him, for I knew him and loved him in the old days. There's not one in a thousand would know him, but I do—it's Hector, sir, is it not?"

"Yes, it's Hector Woodridge, or what's left of him. He's in a bad way, Abe."

"He is, sir."

"And we can't have a doctor to him."

"No, sir, but we'll pull him through. Every man of us will help. Give me permission to tell them. They'll stand by him and Mr. Picton; you need have no fear of that, sir."

"Trust them all; yes, that will be the best," said Ben.

"I'm sure you're right, sir; quite sure."

Captain Ben gave orders for the Sea-mew to leave Torbay, and she was soon moving slowly toward the sea.

He sat beside Hector and listened to his moaning and muttering. He saw the wasted form, the haggard, drawn face, the gray hair, then he noticed the hands and shuddered. What an awful chase that must have been across the moor, bloodhounds on his track, every man's hand against him, no hope, no place to hide in. Yet there must have been one man whose compassion had been aroused on the moor, the man who clothed Hector, when he found

39

him almost naked. Ben vowed when he knew that man's name he should receive his due reward. And there was another man, Brack, honest rough old Brack, with a heart of gold, and the courage of a bulldog. Ben felt it was good to be a sailor and be one of such a class.

Brack must have discovered Hector in Torquay, and hidden him until he could get him on the Sea-mew. Where had he found him? That story was to be told. They were only just in time; Ben thought what might have happened had they missed the Sea-mew and had to return to Torquay, and shuddered. He vowed again that Hector should not be recaptured; no, not if he had to sail the Sea-mew half the world round, and fight for him. It would be weeks, perhaps months, before the fever-stricken man became well, and there was no better hiding-place than the Sea-mew, and no better doctor than the sea and its attendant breeze.

Brack, rowing from the London Belle, saw the Sea-mew moving slowly toward the entrance to the bay.

"He's safe; they'll never part with him. Brack, you're not such a bad sort after all! I wonder where's Hackler got to—perhaps he didn't follow us," thought the old boatman.

He lay on his oars and watched the Sea-mew's lights until they disappeared.

"There's a boat comin' now—wonder if it's him?" he said with a chuckle. "I'm ready for him, anyway."

40

CHAPTER IX

LENISE ELROY

YOU'LL have to hurry," said Hackler impatiently as the seaman slouched round for his boat.

"That's my craft over there; I'll have her alongside in a bit," said the man.

"Can't we take this boat?"

"No, I'll get my own; besides, I'm used to her."

It seemed a long time to Carl before the man brought the boat alongside and he was seated in her.

"Row faster!" said Carl.

"Wait until we're out of the harbor; it's rather dark."

"Go ahead, pull!"

The man obeyed. He was not such a skillful pilot as Brack; as they reached the wall he pulled hard with his right and the boat crashed into the stonework. Carl shot forward, bruising his face; there was a sound of splintering timber; the boatman fell forward. When they recovered, Carl cursed him for a blundering fool. The man found the boat leaked badly; there was nothing for it but to row back as fast as possible and take another.

This caused a delay and enabled Brack to put Hector aboard the Sea-mew and row round by the London Belle in time.

"Who goes there?" shouted Brack.

Carl was sick of the whole business; he was glad to hear Brack's voice. He had been to the London Belle, his story was correct. What a fool he, Carl, had been for his pains!

There was no answer to Brack's hail. Carl said to the man: "Keep on rowing; never mind him."

This did not suit Brack's purpose. He had no desire for Carl to go on board the London Belle; that would upset everything.

Brack went after the boat, quickly overtaking it. By the dim light he saw who was in it.

"You again!" he said with a laugh. "What yer scouring the bay at this time o' night for? Looking for pirates?"

"No, smugglers!" said Carl.

"Hope ye'll catch 'em. Where do they hail from? I thought the days of smuggling in Torbay were over. Better come with me; I'll row you back quicker than him," said Brack.

41

An altercation ensued between the seamen. Brack had insulted Carl's man; the wordy warfare became furious.

"Row back to the harbor!" shouted Carl in a rage. "And you sheer off or it will be the worse for you."

This was all Brack wished to hear. If Hackler returned, there was no danger.

"Keep cool," shouted Brack. "I reckon I'll be home first."

His mother was sitting up anxiously awaiting the news when he came.

"He's got safe away, but we had a narrow squeak for it," he said, and told her what happened.

"I wish our Bill were on the Sea-mew," she said with a sigh.

"Maybe he will be some day, mother," said Brack.

The Sea-mew forged ahead toward the North and Captain Ben watched at Hector's bedside. The unfortunate man slept heavily but uneasily; he groaned and raved incoherently, tossed from side to side, sometimes in danger of falling out of the berth.

Toward six o'clock Ben sent for Abe Glovey, who came and took his place while he went to meet Picton.

Ben had a difficult task before him. He wished to break the news gently; the shock would be great; then they would have to think what was best to be done.

Picton was out early; he had not slept well; strange dreams caused him uneasiness.

"I've had a restless night. You look as though you had," he said to Ben.

"I have; it has been a strange night. I've something to tell you," and he proceeded to explain about Brack coming to the yacht.

"What on earth did he want at that hour of the night?" said Picton.

"He brought some one to see me."

Picton was surprised.

"Who was it?"

"A man," said Ben. He was not a good hand at this sort of thing; he wanted to blurt it all out in his blunt way.

Picton smiled.

"Don't beat about the bush, Ben; you can't do it."

"That's a fact, I can't. You'll stand a shock, Picton, a very great shock."

"Is it tremendous?"

"Yes," said Ben seriously. "The man Brack brought here last night is aboard now; he's asleep in my cabin; he is very ill; he has suffered a lot; he will require a great deal of care. We shall have to be very careful."

42

Picton looked at him wonderingly. Gradually a light broke in upon him; he turned pale and felt giddy. Ever since the boom of the gun startled him he had had Hector in his mind.

"Was it Hector who escaped?" he asked.

Ben nodded.

"Was it Hector Brack brought to the Sea-mew?"

Again Ben nodded.

"Let us go to him," said Picton.

Ben wondered at his taking it so calmly, but he knew the strain must be great. They went to Ben's cabin.

"Glovey's inside; I'll send him out," said Ben.

When the man was gone Picton stepped inside and looked at his brother with tears in his eyes.

"What a wreck, Ben; it's awful."

Captain Ben turned away his head. There are some things worse than death to look upon, cause more sorrow and pain.

Hector lay on his back. His face told a tale of misery such as few care to hear, and none to suffer.

"Leave me, Ben; I'd rather bear this alone; I may get used to it in time," said Picton in a hollow voice.

Ben put his hand on the younger man's shoulder for a moment, then went out of the cabin; he never wished to feel again as he felt then, in the whole course of his life. Picton watched Hector, heard his ravings, shuddered at them, and wondered how it were possible for a man to suffer so much and live. He stayed there over two hours, and what his thoughts were during that time no one knew; there was, however, throughout, one predominant resolve: Hector should never go back to Dartmoor. He would sooner see him dead; it would be more merciful. What roused Picton was the thought of the woman who had done this thing; he held her responsible. She was older than Hector, a woman subtle, versed in the wiles of the world, and she had lured him to destruction. If ever a woman should suffer she ought. He wondered how she would feel if she stood where he stood now, looking down at the awful disaster of this man's life. Would she smile? She might; he thought she would; he believed at that moment she was the worst woman he had ever heard of. She must pay the penalty sooner or later; no atonement on her part could wash out that. These thoughts stifled him; he opened the door for fresh air. Ben's cabin was on deck; as the light streamed in Hector awoke. Before Picton realized what had happened his brother sprang from the berth, rushed past him, and had Abe Glovey not caught him round the waist would have flung himself overboard.

43

With difficulty they carried him, struggling, back to the cabin, and laid him down exhausted.

"He's mad," said Picton.

"Temporarily, but we'll cure all that. I'm a bit of a doctor; leave him to me," said Ben, trying to make the best of it.

"What are we to do?" asked Picton.

"You mean about concealing him?"

"Yes."

Ben said he had taken Abe Glovey into his confidence, and they had decided the whole of the crew should know the facts.

"Will it be safe?" asked Picton.

"I am sure of it; they are all real good fellows, and it is our only chance."

"You must call them together and explain it all," said Picton.

Ben said he would, and went on: "This is the opportunity we have waited for—Hector's escape. How fortunate we came here! Providence had a hand in this, it's more than mere coincidence, and as Providence helps those who help themselves we must lend a hand. When Hector recovers, it will be some weeks; he must remain on the Sea-mew until he becomes a changed man. In twelve months no one will know him who has seen him now; the change will be wonderful, and it will be quite as wonderful a change from what he was before the trial. Hector Woodridge must cease to exist; he is dead; his body was never found on the Moor because he probably fell down some disused mine or was drowned in a still pond. That way safety lies, but there may be one stumbling block."

"What is that?" asked Picton.

"Hector's desire to prove his innocence," said Ben.

"He must be persuaded that will be easier to do if it is thought he is dead; we must try and do it."

"We have tried; there is only one person in the world who can prove his innocence," said Ben.

"Lenise Elroy," said Picton.

"Yes, Lenise Elroy. There were three persons in the room at the time: Raoul Elroy, Lenise Elroy, and Hector," said Ben.

"Hector said at the trial the weapon went off in a struggle," said Picton.

"Lenise Elroy, with apparent reluctance, said Hector shot her husband," said Ben.

"If this were not true, why did she say it?" asked Picton.

"She may have thought it true. Heaven knows what is in the mind of a woman like that! But the truth will come out some day."

"Still, she ought to have shielded him, corroborated his story that it was an accident," said Picton.

44

"The strangest part of the whole thing is that Hector has not told even you what actually happened," said Ben.

"And I don't believe he will," said Picton.

CHAPTER X

HAVERTON

WHEN the Sea-mew arrived at Bridlington Bay Hector Woodridge lay at death's door, but the fever had somewhat abated and the ravings ceased. He was completely exhausted, worn out, and Picton doubted if he would have strength to struggle back to life.

Captain Ben had seen a good deal of illness and was confident he could pull Hector round in time, but he said it would take many weeks.

What was to be done? Picton could not remain on the Sea-mew; his absence would be noted at Haverton, where Brant Blackett was busy with the horses and expecting his arrival daily.

"Abe Glovey is a good seaman, quite capable of looking after the Sea-mew," said Ben. "There is no reason why she should not remain here for a time; there will be nothing unusual about it. I will stay until Hector is convalescent, or nearly so, and then join you at Haverton. Glovey can take the Sea-mew short cruises; when they are away from the coast Hector can come on deck freely without danger. Leave it all to me; I'll explain to him when he is well enough."

Picton thought this the best thing they could do.

He went ashore at Bridlington and from there traveled to Haverton. He knew he was running a grave risk in having Hector on board his yacht. He cared very little about that; all he wanted was for his brother to get well. He was certain no one would recognize him, he was so changed. It was a long, tedious journey to Haverton, and Picton was glad when it was over, and he was in his own house again.

Mrs. Yeoman, the housekeeper, was surprised not to see Captain Bruce; he was seldom away from Picton. He explained in answer to her question that the Captain had remained on the Sea-mew to see to some repairs in the engineers' department. This only half satisfied her; she knew McTavish was a capable man and could look after repairs himself. She had a very kindly feeling toward Jack McTavish, who sometimes came to Haverton and was not at all averse to a mild flirtation with the buxom, comely widow.

When she saw Blackett she asked him what he thought about it.

"Why hasn't the Captain come with him? It's all moonshine his staying on the Sea-mew to see to repairs in the engine room. Mac's quite good enough for that job," she said.

"It's none of your business, anyway," said Brant; "and as for McTavish, you're prejudiced in his favor—I shouldn't wonder if you aren't Sarah McTavish some day."

"Nonsense, Brant! I've had one dose of married life; I don't want to try it again," she said.

"Give the poor man a chance; he's only one thing against him," said the trainer.

"And pray what's that?" she asked.

"His name."

"Jack McTavish. I reckon it's the equal of Brant Blackett, anyway," she said.

He laughed as he answered: "You're always a bit touchy where the McTavish is concerned. I wish you luck with him, Sarah. We'll see you a Highland chieftainess before many months are passed. I'll put myself in training and dance a reel after the ceremony's over."

"You're old enough to know better, and you ought to have more sense," she snapped, and walked away.

Picton had been at Haverton a week and still Captain Ben did not come. He was anxious, but knew he could do no good if he went to the yacht; he was better away. He rode several of the horses at work to keep himself occupied, and was constantly roaming about the estate. He felt lonely; he missed Ben sadly; he was such excellent company.

Haverton was a large mansion situated in one of the most beautiful districts in Yorkshire. The mansion had an aspect of gentility, and its various forms of architecture made it doubly interesting. The strong tower on the North East dated from Plantagenet times, and was a fine example of those peel towers on the border, of which the most southern are in the north of Yorkshire. The west side was in the Tudor times, showing the domestic architecture of the period. The two towers were commanding features of the fine old mansion. The gardens were lovely old-world places; clipped yews and flower beds intermingled on the south terrace The entrance was imposing and the gates were always open, as though the visitors were expected; the hospitality of Haverton was proverbial, even in such a county as Yorkshire.

Picton was very proud of the old mansion, which had been in the possession of the Woodridges for many generations. He loved the glorious park with its magnificent trees, and undulating stretches of land. Oaks of great age, with their knotted arms outstretched, studded the landscape in all directions. There was a

47

large lake, a mile long, half a mile wide, and in it were pike of great size and weight. In the river Aver, which flowed through the park, were trout, perch, grayling, and many other kinds of fish, and here they were safe from the voracious pike in the lake. Picton was a good angler, and he loved to have a tussle with a twenty-four-pound pike, or a thirty-one-pound trout in the river. He was the owner of the land for many miles round, numerous farms, which had been in the same families for ages, and the famous downs of Haverton, where so many good horses had been trained. These downs were magnificent galloping grounds, and there was a clear stretch of three miles straight—small wonder that Brant Blackett turned out some good stayers.

Picton gloried in a good gallop on the downs, where the wind whistled in freedom, and where there was no occasion to ease a horse until he had done a four- or five-mile burst.

He was happy at Haverton—at least he always appeared to be—but there was one thing cast a gloom over the place at all times: that was the Admiral's death, and the cause of it—Hector's sentence to penal servitude, after his reprieve. This was why Picton did not care to be alone in the great house, why he always wished Captain Ben to be with him. He had many friends who came to see him, but his best friend next to Ben was Dick Langford, and he was far away in Devonshire. Sarah Yeoman, at the end of a week, took it upon herself to speak to Picton.

"You're lonely, sir; you're brooding. It's not good for young folks to brood. Wait till you're my age; then you can start if you are so minded. The Captain ought to come, sir. He's been gallivanting on the Sea-mew long enough; I hope there's not a lady in the case, Mr. Picton," she said.

Mrs. Yeoman was privileged; she had been at Haverton since she came as a girl over thirty years ago and by sheer worth had risen to the position of housekeeper, and ruler, at Haverton. Her husband had been a groom there. Sarah Yeoman practically ruled everybody and everything at Haverton; even Robert Rose, the butler, Amos Kidd, the head gardener, and all the rest of the male and female kind bowed down to her will. They bowed but did not worship; some of the maids—there were four—would have liked to pull her back hair at times and scratch her, but Sarah, although aware some feeling of this sort existed, went on her way serene and calm, knowing she was doing her duty. There was one thing about her: she was just, she held an even balance when there was a dispute; and Fanny, the head housemaid, who at times almost hated her, said she'd trust Sarah Yeoman under any circumstances to arrive at a right decision. She was slow to anger but when roused "all hands" fled from her wrath. With all her faults, there could have been no better woman chosen to take the helm at Haverton. She was loyal to the backbone; she considered the Woodridges the best family in Yorkshire, or any other shire. She felt the blow when Hector was condemned, and had not forgotten it, never would forget. She loved both boys in her motherly way, and, although Picton was her favorite, she held Hector in high esteem. She was surprised at Hector's falling a victim to a woman, she would not have been surprised had Picton done so.

"No, I don't think there's a lady in the case," replied Picton, smiling. "At least I am not aware of it."

"Sailors are sly," she said.

"I thought Captain Ben was a favorite of yours," he said.

"So he is, but sailors are sailors all the same, and there's no telling what he's up to on board the Sea-mew," she said.

Picton thought she would be astonished if she knew what Captain Ben was up to.

"I think I'll go to Bridlington to-morrow and see him," he said.

"If you do, bring him back with you."

"I will if possible."

"Why should it not be possible? What's to hinder him from coming?" she asked.

They would need her help later on, when Hector came to Haverton; he might as well tell her now: she was thoroughly trustworthy.

"A strange thing happened when we were at Torquay," said Picton.

She waited for him to go on.

"Late one night, just before we sailed, an old boatman rowed across the bay to the Sea-mew bringing a man with him."

"Well?" she said anxiously.

"Captain Ben was on deck, the boatman hailed him and said the man had come to see me. Ben asked his name, it was not given, but the boatman—Brack we call him—implored him to permit the man to go on board. So earnestly did he plead that Ben opened the gangway and let down the steps. The man no sooner set foot on them than Brack cleared away as fast as he could. The man came on deck, he seemed dazed, behaved like a madman. He flung himself on Ben, who easily held him back, the poor fellow was terribly weak and starved. Ben looked into his face, the man looked back; they recognized each other. That man is on the Sea-mew now. Captain Ben is watching over him, nursing him back to life and sanity. A great and grave task lies before us. We have to shield this man, hide him, until such time as he can come ashore without danger of being recognized. There was an escape from Dartmoor when we were at Torquay, Sarah."

She gasped; she felt faint; she pulled herself together.

"An escape from Dartmoor—not——"

"Hector. He is on the Sea-mew. That is why Captain Ben is not here," said Picton.

CHAPTER XI

TEARAWAY AND OTHERS

THERE was no occasion for Picton to travel to Bridlington. Captain Ben arrived next day and was very pleased to see him.

"He's much better," said Ben; "making a wonderful recovery. He's quite sane, remembers everything, but his health is terribly shattered and a long rest on the Sea-mew will do him a world of good. He has no desire to come to Haverton, or to leave the yacht; he thinks he is safer where he is, and he is right. There was no need to caution him to be careful, he knows what it means for all of us if there is the slightest suspicion about the Sea-mew. Glovey will attend to him, so will Mac, and the crew to a man have sworn to keep everything secret. Don't worry yourself about it, Picton; it will do no good; and I will return in a week or so to see how he is going on."

"Mrs. Yeoman knows," said Picton.

"She can be trusted, and it is better she should; it will prepare her for his coming," said Ben.

It was no use worrying, as Ben said, and as Brant Blackett was anxious to put the horses through the mill, several trials took place on the moor.

Tearaway proved herself a veritable flyer; she easily disposed of the lot pitted against her, and fully bore out the trainer's opinion of her, that she was as fast as the wind. She was a beautiful mare, black as coal, not a white speck on her, and stood sixteen hands high. No fault could be found with her; she was sound in her wind and limb, possessed terrific speed and was also a stayer. Blackett idolized her; he was desperately cut up that she had not been entered in any of the classic events, with the exception of the St. Leger. How she came to be entered in the great Doncaster race was peculiar. Her breeder, a Yorkshire squire, always entered his youngsters freely in the classic races. Somehow Tearaway had been overlooked until the last moment and a telegram was sent to enter the filly by King Charles—Far Away, in the St. Leger only. This was Tearaway, who was named afterward.

Picton bought her at the sales at Doncaster for five hundred guineas, at which price she was a bargain.

She ran only once as a two-year-old because Blackett saw she

51

was growing fast and required time; to hurry her thus early in her career might, he said, ruin her.

Picton was immensely proud of her, and desirous of bringing off a great coup by winning the St. Leger. It had been the Admiral's ambition to win the Doncaster event, and more than once he had been within an ace of doing so. Every Yorkshire owner of horses, on any pretensions to a large scale, is anxious to win the Leger, the greatest race in the North.

Tearaway was practically an unknown quantity and Picton decided she should not run in public before September. With some fillies this would have been a risky policy to pursue, but Tearaway was so quiet and docile that there was no fear of her being frightened by a crowd, no matter how large, or by any amount of noise. The trainer agreed with this plan: Blackett was quite as anxious to win a Leger as his master. He was a Yorkshireman, and patriotism was strong within him.

Brant Blackett was intended by his father for an auctioneer and had been sent to a local firm in Whitby. He hated office work and was always slipping away and going out to sea on one of the fishing boats. The firm declined to have anything to do with him, and in some way or other he drifted to Middleham and took a situation in a racing stable. He was small, weighed under eight stone, and soon learned to ride well. He never rode in public but was considered as good as the best of them in getting the strength of a trial. He was recommended to the Admiral, when he wanted a private trainer, and came to Haverton, where he had been for many years. He was much attached to the family, and the place, and, like the rest of them, he was cut up over Hector Woodridge's trial. He had won many races during the time he had been at Haverton, but vowed no such flier had been in his hands as Tearaway. He was fond of the breed, and fond of the mare, and she repaid his kindness by being as obedient as a child.

"She's the sweetest-tempered filly I ever handled," he said. "Her temper's just lovely. She never flares up, or misbehaves; a perfect lady, that's what she is."

Everybody who saw the filly agreed with him, and in the Haverton district Tearaway was regarded as a good thing for the St. Leger.

"It's a long way off to September," said Picton as he and Ben sat on their hacks and looked at her after a morning gallop. She had been two miles at a fast pace and pulled up without the slightest sign of blowing. Her glorious black coat shone like satin in the sunlight; she tossed her head proudly, looking round with intelligent eyes that took in all her surroundings.

52

"No need to hurry her," said the trainer; "and there's nothing will happen to her, I'm sure. A sounder mare never stepped."

"We have hardly anything good enough to try her," said Picton.

"That's a fact," said Blackett. "It takes something out of the common to extend her."

There were a dozen horses at work, some cantering, others having spins over five and six furlongs.

As Picton rode back with Ben and the trainer he said: "What with one thing and another I forgot to tell you Mr. Langford is sending The Rascal here and he says I am at liberty to do what I like with him. He's a real good 'chaser, the same I won the double on at Torquay. It would be rather a joke if we won the St. Leger with Tearaway, and the National with The Rascal. I wonder if a trainer ever accomplished that feat?" said Picton, smiling.

"Never heard of it," said Blackett; "but I don't see why it should not be done. We've a pretty good schooling ground here."

"The Rascal is one of the best horses I have ridden over fences. He's a bit queer-tempered, but once he settles down to his work you can depend upon him to do his best," said Picton.

"Then, if he'll do that, he must be a good horse no matter what his temper may be," said the trainer.

During the week The Rascal arrived at Haverton and the white-faced chestnut created a favorable impression.

Picton found the same difficulty in mounting him, but once in the saddle all went well, and the way the horse took the stiffish fences on the Haverton schooling ground convinced the trainer there was a good race in him; but whether The Rascal was up to National form was another matter.

Picton wrote to Dick Langford, stating The Rascal had arrived safely, and saying he wished he, Dick, had come with him.

When Dick received this letter he said to his sister: "This is as good as an invitation. I'll avail myself of it and go down to Haverton for a few days. You don't mind, Rita?"

"Indeed, no; I think Mr. Woodridge is a very good friend," she replied.

"He is, and he'll make a very decent sort of brother-in-law," said Dick.

"Don't be silly," said Rita, her cheeks glowing.

"Is it silly? Not a bit of it—you know it's not. Picton's fond of you, and you're fond of him—that ends the matter. I wonder he hasn't asked you before."

"Asked what?"

"To be his wife."

Rita laughed as she said: "I think you spoilt an opportunity when you called to us in the garden that night. You remember?"

"Yes, I remember, and I also recollect I thought what a fool I was at the time," he said.

Picton was glad when Dick Langford arrived at Haverton; it gave Ben a chance to go back to the Sea-mew for a few days.

Dick always enjoyed a visit here, and small wonder, for such a lovely place could not fail to attract. He was fond of horses and Brant Blackett liked him.

"I hate showing a fellow round who pretends he knows a heap and knows nothing," said the trainer. "With Mr. Langford it's different; he's a very fair judge, and he's willing to learn; he's never cocksure about anything. He makes some shrewd remarks too, and he's clever—yes, I like Mr. Langford; there's grit in him."

Mrs. Yeoman gave Dick the hall-mark of her approval.

"He's a cheerful soul, not given to moping, and he's easily pleased; he always cheers Mr. Picton up, and he wants it at times— more than ever now," she thought.

It had come as a shock to her when Picton told her Hector had escaped and was on board the Sea-mew. She wondered if he were safe there. Picton told her Hector would be so changed when he left the yacht that no one would recognize him, and that he would change his name. Hector Woodridge would be dead to the world.

"Unless he can prove his innocence," he said.

"Oh, I wish that could be done!" she said. "Some day I think it will come to pass. He's innocent, I'm sure of it. Do you know what I think, Mr. Picton?"

"No; what is it?"

"I believe Mrs. Elroy killed her husband."

"Good heavens!" exclaimed Picton. "What makes you think that?"

"I read every scrap of evidence at the trial. I am almost certain Mr. Hector was shielding her; he's just the sort."

"If your surmise is correct his innocence will never come to light, because he will never betray her," said Picton.

"Perhaps not, but she can't stand that on her conscience forever, she'll have to confess sooner or later, the burden is more than any woman or man can bear," she said.

"She may have done it," said Picton. "Her punishment must already be great if she did."

"If I were Mr. Hector, I'd seek her out and make her own up to it," she said.

"That's all very well, but you may be mistaken. In any case it is in Hector's hands, and he will not allow any one to interfere," said Picton.

CHAPTER XII

"I THINK HE'S DEAD"

IT was Lenise Elroy who was supping at the Torbay Hotel when Hector Woodridge looked through the chink in the blind and saw her with her friends. The man who brought her the wrap to put on her shoulders was Fletcher Denyer.

Denyer lived mainly on his wits. He was a dark, handsome man, about ten years younger than Mrs. Elroy, and made her acquaintance some two years back at a ball at a large London hotel. He was a man likely to attract such a woman. He was unscrupulous; of his morals the less said the better; he possessed unlimited confidence in himself. Who he was, or where he came from, no one appeared to know, but he had wormed himself into a certain class of society, had become known on the racecourse, and in financial circles, and acted as a kind of tout to more than one firm of wine merchants, also to a big turf commission agent, who treated him liberally when he introduced business. His address was Marine View, Hove, Brighton, and he was frequently to be seen in the gay city by the sea.

Marine View was a small house off one of the main streets, comfortably furnished, and Denyer was the sole tenant. Two half caste servants, a man and his wife, looked after the place. The man's name was Antonio Tobasco, his wife's Lucille, and they knew more about their master than any one.

Tobasco seemed devoted to Denyer; so did his wife; they attended to his wants, and looked after the house during his absence. Tobasco's father was an Italian emigrant who went to America in the fifties, and gradually drifted to Mexico, where he married a native woman. Lucille's mother was an Italian, her father a dark man in the Southern States. There was plenty of black blood in them, and with it mingled a certain amount of treachery. Denyer had lived in Mexico; it was here he became acquainted with them, through Lucille, whom at one time he admired—it was his money that gave Tobasco the chance to marry her, but the man did not know of the relations which at one time existed between Denyer and Lucille. She was quite contented to marry him, and the union had proved satisfactory for several years.

It was Lucille who persuaded Denyer to bring them to

England with him. At first he refused, but she knew how to handle him and succeeded in having her way.

Lenise Elroy had seen Hector's face at the window, just a glimpse, but sufficient to frighten her. She thought she recognized him, then wondered why she had been such a fool; he was safe in Dartmoor, and not likely to come out again. At the same time she could not get rid of the impression, nor could she make an excuse for her sudden alarm.

She came to Torquay with Denyer at his request; he said he wanted a change, and her society. There was no question of love on his side, although Lenise was a handsome woman, but he was to a certain extent infatuated with her, and proud of being seen in her company. What her feelings were toward him she hardly knew. She was at a critical age, when a woman sometimes loses her head over a man much younger than herself. She would have been very sorry to lose Denyer's friendship, but she had no intention of letting her inclinations run away with her common sense. She kept on the right side, there was nothing wrong between them; they were familiar, but it had been carried no farther, and she was determined to be his wife, if she wished—at present she did not wish it.

She tormented him, but at the same time attracted him; moreover, she was useful to him. She had a settled income, he had not; occasionally he found himself short of money, hard up. She helped him, he pocketed the cash and felt grateful for a few days. She did not despise him for taking the money from her; she wished to bind him to her, and this was a sure way.

It was during her brief stay at Torquay that Lenise Elroy came across Brack. She was fond of the sea, had a liking for rowing in small boats.

"Can't understand what you see in 'em," said Denyer; "beastly cockly things, might go over at any moment."

"Well, I do like them, and I'm not going to explain why. If you don't care to go out, stay here until I come back; I'm going to have a row round the men-of-war," she said.

"Please yourself, but it's a waste of time. Why not go for a motor drive instead?"

"I prefer the row; you take the motor."

"I will. Brady's doing business, so I'll take his wife for a spin; she's good company."

"Very," said Lenise. "She's not at all a bad sort."

She knew very well Mrs. Brady would not go out alone with him; if he didn't know it, he was not quite so wide awake as she imagined.

56

She went to the harbor, and, seeing Brack, took a fancy to him.

"Want to go for a row?" he asked.

"Yes, round the warships."

"I'm yer man. I get a lot of patronage from ladies; they're safe with me, I'm a steady goin' old 'un."

He took his blackened pipe out of his mouth and slipped it into his pocket.

"This is my boat, The Dart," he said. "Wait till I put the cushion right for you."

She got in. Brack thought what a handsome woman she was.

He was about to push off when he looked up and saw Carl Hackler.

"So yer here still, messin' about! Wonder yer not tired of it," he said.

"I am," said Carl. "Dead tired of it! Nothing can be done here. My belief is he's dead."

"And mine too; he couldn't have stood it all this time, wandering about the moor," Brack said.

When they were out in the bay she asked:

"Who is dead? What were you talking about?"

"It's a long story, mum, a sad story; I don't suppose it would interest you."

"Who was that man on the quay?" she asked.

"He's from Dartmoor, from the prison," said Brack.

He did not see the look of interest on her face as he spoke.

"A warder?" she asked.

"Not exactly that; I fancy he's one of the fellows turned on for special duty at times."

"And what is he doing at Torquay?"

"A week or so back a man escaped from Dartmoor prison. They've not caught him yet; it's my opinion they never will," he answered with a chuckle.

She felt that peculiar feeling come over that she experienced when she fancied she saw Hector's face looking through the window of the hotel.

"What nonsense!" she thought. "There are hundreds of prisoners there; why should he be the one to escape?"

She was restless, all the same, and wished Brack would tell her more.

"I suppose it is no uncommon thing for a prisoner to escape?" she asked.

"No; they do a bolt sometimes. They're generally caught inside twenty-four hours."

"But this man is not taken?"

"No, and Hackler's been mooning about Torquay looking for him for a week, just as though the fellow would be likely to come here," said Brack.

"I wonder who he was?"

"Don't know, but he was a good plucked 'un," said Brack, and proceeded to tell her all about the throttling of the hound.

"He must be a very desperate character," she said.

"It's enough to make a man desperate," said Brack.

"What was he in prison for?" she asked.

"Murder, so I've heard," said Brack.

She started.

"What murder, where?"

"Somewhere up in Yorkshire, I believe," said Brack, who was now watching her. He saw her turn pale and clutch the side of the boat with one hand.

"Takes an uncommon interest in it," he thought. "Wonder who she is?"

"Do you know anything about the murder—the trial I mean? You come from Yorkshire, do you not—I can tell by your accent," she said with a faint attempt at a smile.

"Yes, I'm fra Yorkshire," said Brack. "Used to be at Scarborough some years ago."

"I come from Yorkshire too," she said. "I remember some years ago there was a celebrated trial there, a murder case, the man who was convicted shot the husband of some lady he had been compromised with. It was a very sad case, a very old Yorkshire family, I forget the name, it was Wood something—oh, I have it, Woodridge, that's it. Do you recollect it?"

Brack was on the alert. She knew a good deal more about it than she pretended; he was sure of it. Who was she?

"I remember it; most folks up our way will remember it to their dying day," he said.

"Why?"

"Because no one believed him guilty."

"But he was found guilty and sentenced."

"Many an innocent man suffers for another's crime," said Brack.

"Perhaps it was this man who escaped," she said.

"If it were, the poor fellow's dead by now," said Brack. "They did say at the time it was the woman, the wife, that got him into his trouble. Women's generally at the bottom of these things. I believe she was a mighty fine woman too; but she must have been wicked."

Lenise was restless.

58

"Don't you think we had better put back?" she said.

"I thought you wanted to row round the men-o'-war," he said.

"It is too far; I want to be back for lunch."

"Shall I turn round?"

"Yes, please."

"Do you think they'll catch the man who escaped?" she asked before they reached the landing steps.

"I think he's dead or they'd have got him afore now," said Brack.

She gave a sigh of relief, as she handed him half a sovereign.

"I haven't got any change," said Brack.

"You can keep that; you interested me in your conversation. What did you say was the name of the man from the prison?"

"Carl Hackler," said Brack.

"Thank you; if I wish to go out again I will take your boat."

"Very good, my lady, always at your service," said Brack; adding to himself, "I'd like to find out who she is, and why she's so mighty interested in it all."

59

CHAPTER XIII

A WOMAN'S FEAR

LENISE ELROY was troubled; she felt uneasy, afraid of something, she hardly knew what; she had a presentiment that a calamity hung over her, that much trouble was in store.

Fletcher Denyer was irritated. She was not at all like the gay woman of a few days back; what ailed her? He questioned her, received no satisfactory reply.

"I want to go to town," he said.

"I don't; I like being here."

"But I must return to London, I have a lot of business to see to."

She smiled; when he talked about business it amused her.

He noticed it and said angrily: "You never think I do anything in the way of business."

"I judge by results," she answered.

"And I don't show any, is that it?"

She nodded.

"Look here, Len, we've been together for a couple of years and been good friends; we don't want to quarrel now."

"I'm sure I've no wish to do so."

"There's a good deal more in me than you imagine. Why didn't you speculate in those Mexican shares I told you about? You'd have made a pile."

"I should; you were right in that instance. It has always struck me you know a good deal about Mexico."

"Perhaps I do; it's a great country, I'm told."

"I suppose you have not been there?" she said.

"If I had, I should probably be better off."

"If you must go to London, go. I'll follow in a few days," she said.

"You seem to have suddenly taken an interest in the place."

"I have, I like it. It is my first visit. I think it beautiful," she said.

He wondered why she wished to remain, but did not question her further. In the afternoon he went to London. She was glad to be alone; she wanted to be quiet and think. Supposing Hector Woodridge had escaped from Dartmoor, and was not dead, what would happen? What would he do to her? She trembled, felt faint;

there was no telling to what lengths such a man infuriated at the cruelty and misery he had suffered, might go. She must find out more about it. The man to see was Carl Hackler, but how to approach him?

She meant to converse with him at any cost, and went out with that intention.

Carl had nothing to do but idle time away; he was quite certain the prisoner had either got clear off, or was lying dead on the moor. He saw Mrs. Elroy coming toward him, and recognized her as the lady Brack had taken out in his boat. She evidently intended speaking to him.

"You are Mr. Hackler, I believe?" she asked.

"I am; at your service."

"The boatman told me who you were. You come from the prison at Dartmoor?"

"I do."

"A man has escaped, I want to know more about it. The boatman gave me to understand he was tried for murder in Yorkshire some years ago. If this is the man who escaped I know him, I know the family," she said.

"What name?" asked Hackler.

"Woodridge. Hector Woodridge," she said.

"I believe it's the same man," said Hackler, interested.

"Will he be caught?"

"If he's alive he's sure to be taken."

"But you think it probable he is dead?" she questioned.

"I think it quite possible."

"Are you here on the lookout for him?"

"Yes."

"Surely he would not be likely to come to Torquay."

"I don't know so much about that. You see he might be able to get away by sea if he had friends, or some one willing to help him," said Hackler.

"Who would help him? The risk would be too great."

"There's many men take risks for each other. You seem interested in him."

"I am. I know him, a dangerous man, I should not care to meet him again," she said.

"He had not that reputation at Dartmoor. He was quiet and inoffensive, about the last man we'd have thought would try to escape," he said.

"And you have no doubt he is Hector Woodridge?"

"No, I don't think there's much doubt about that; in fact none at all. It is improbable he will meet you again. Even if he has got away he'll go out of the country into some safe hiding-place; he's not likely to roam about England," he said.

She thanked him, asked him to accept a sovereign, which he did not refuse.

Carl Hackler watched her as she walked away; she looked stately, carried herself well, what he called a "stunner."

Carl wondered why she was so anxious to find out who the escaped prisoner was. She must have some personal interest in him; she did not seem like a woman who wasted her time over trifles. He determined to see Brack and hear what he had to say about the lady. He had a good deal of regard for Brack, also a shrewd idea that in some way or another the boatman had the better of him.

Brack was nothing loath to chat when Carl came up.

"All the ladies seem fond of you, Brack," he said.

"Yes, I don't say as they're not; I often has ladies in my boat," he said.

"Rather a smart woman you took out to-day."

"A very pretty craft, built on fine lines," said Brack.

"I've had a talk with her. She's interested in the man I'm on the lookout for."

"Is she?"

"You know she is. Didn't she speak about him when you took her out?"

"Maybe she did, maybe she didn't."

Carl laughed.

"You're a sly old sea dog," he said. "Now Brack, listen to me. That lady is interested in Hector Woodridge, No. 832; that's his name, certain of it, no mistake. Another thing, she's afraid of him; afraid he'll do her some bodily harm if he comes across her. Now why should he? There must be some good reason."

"Afraid of him, is she? By gad, I thought the same thing."

"Then you talked about him in the boat?"

"Yes, that's so."

"What did she say?"

"Not much; she knew the family, his family, knew all about the trial."

"Did she now? What was the woman like?"

"Which woman?"

"The wife of the man Woodridge shot."

Brack was thoughtful.

"What yer drivin' at, Carl, my boy?"

"I've got a kind of notion she must have been mixed up in the case," said Carl.

"There was only one woman in it—the wife," said Brack. "Gosh!" he exclaimed, and looked at Carl with a startled expression.

"Well?" said Carl.

"I thought I'd seen her face somewhere afore, pictures of her, photos, or something."

"Yes; go on."

"I may be mistaken; I'd not like to say as much without being certain."

"You can trust me; it shall go no farther."

"She's like the wife, the woman whose husband he shot," said Brack.

"You've hit it," said Carl. "That accounts for it; she is the woman, no doubt."

"Don't hurry; it may be only a likeness."

"You'd not have remembered it if she'd not been the woman," said Carl. "It's stuck in your memory."

"If she's the one, no wonder she's afraid to meet him—he'd do for her."

"I don't think so. He must have been precious fond of her, or he'd never have done time for her."

"Come home with me and have a talk," said Brack, and Carl went.

Mrs. Elroy found it slow at night, but her thoughts were busy. She was restless, ate very little dinner, hardly spoke to Mrs. Brady, or her husband, and left them as soon as she could decently do so.

"Seems out of sorts," said Brady.

"Fletcher Denyer has gone to town," was Mrs. Brady's comment, and she spoke as though that explained everything.

"Do you think she's fond of him?" he asked.

"Yes, but she hardly knows it."

"Is he fond of her?"

"He's not in love with her; he's infatuated, that's all. Lenise has a way with the men that's hard to resist," she said.

Mrs. Elroy, for want of something better to do, looked over some back copies of the Torquay Times, and came across an account of the races. She saw Picton Woodridge had ridden four winners, which surprised her not a little; she had not seen him for years, had no desire to meet him.

Then she read about the escape from Dartmoor; there was not much about it, she gleaned very little fresh information.

A paragraph that attracted her close attention was about Picton Woodridge's yacht, the Sea-mew. A description of it was given and at the end it stated, "She left the bay during the night, her departure was rather unexpected."

Picton Woodridge's yacht in Torbay at the time Hector escaped from Dartmoor. Was this a coincidence, or was it part of a well-laid plan? She shivered, felt cold, a chill passed over her. She rang the bell and ordered a brandy; this put new life into her for the moment. Her brain worked actively; she was piecing things together. The Sea-mew left in the night unexpectedly. Why? Had Hector Woodridge contrived to board her? Had Picton and Captain Ben Bruce helped him?

The thought tormented her, she could not sleep, she tossed uneasily on her bed.

"He's dead! Hackler says so, the boatman says so; he could not live on the moor. It is impossible. How could he reach the Sea-mew? Supposing he seeks me out, what would he do?"

A cold perspiration broke out over her body.

"He'd kill me if I didn't speak," she said with a shudder.

64

CHAPTER XIV

NOT RECOGNIZED

THE Sea-mew cruised about from one place to another and Hector Woodridge recovered his health and strength; but he was a changed man. Even Picton thought it difficult to recognize him; he would not have done so had he met him in the street.

Captain Ben said: "It is quite safe for you to go ashore. You are supposed to be dead; you must take another name."

"William Rolfe—how will that do?" said Hector.

"As good as any other," said Picton. "We'll test it. You come to Haverton as William Rolfe to look at the horses, and if Sarah Yeoman and Blackett don't recognize you it will be proof positive there is no danger."

It was early in August when Hector Woodridge, as William Rolfe, came to Haverton. Mrs. Yeoman did not recognize him, nor did the trainer, although the former thought his face familiar.

The change in Hector was extraordinary. Not only was his appearance entirely different, but his voice, manner, everything about him was that of another man.

Mrs. Yeoman and Blackett were not enlightened as to his identity. Hector was glad they did not recognize him; he was careful to give them no clue to his identity, although occasionally when off his guard he almost betrayed himself by showing his knowledge of the house and its surroundings. Amos Kidd, the head gardener, as he saw him walking about, thought: "He must have been here before, but I don't recollect seeing him."

It was a sore trial to him to come back to the old home as a stranger. Everything revived recollections of the misery he had caused, and of the Admiral's death, and at last these became so vivid and painful that he told Picton he could stand it no longer.

"I shall go mad if I stay here," he said. "I must get away."

"Where will you go?" asked Picton.

"To London for a time; it is a safe place—such a vast crowd—and probably I am forgotten at Dartmoor. There is an advantage in being dead, is there not?" he said, smiling grimly.

"Perhaps it will be for the best. In London you will see so many sights, your attention will be taken away from the past. I quite understand how you feel about Haverton, but you will grow out of it in time," said Picton.

"Never; at least not until my innocence is proved."

"You think it will be?"

"Yes, it must; I mean to prove it."

"How?"

"Leave that to me. I have a plan which may prove successful, but it will be risky; everything will depend on the first bold step."

"Don't rush into danger," said Picton. "Where's the use? You may fail; you may be recognized; and then, think what would follow."

"You fear I might be sent back to prison," he said, smiling. "There is no fear of that. I promise you I will never go back to Dartmoor."

"You must have all the money you require, Hector," said his brother.

"I shall want money; there is plenty for both."

"Ample; it costs a lot to keep up Haverton, but half of what I have is yours."

"Too generous, Pic; you always were. I shall not want half, nothing like it. Place a few thousands to my credit in a London bank."

"That would not be safe. I will draw ten thousand pounds in notes, and you can use it as you think best," said Picton.

"Very well. That is a large sum, but I shall probably require it. The scheme I have in my mind will cost money, a lot of it, but I'd sacrifice all I have to prove my innocence," said Hector.

"And I will help you. I want to keep up Haverton, but you shall have the rest. I'll tell you what. Hector, I'm going to back Tearaway to win a fortune in the St. Leger. Already money is going on at forty to one; I may get a thousand on at that price, perhaps more," said Picton.

"I'd like to see her have a spin before I leave," said Hector.

"And you shall. Blackett has obtained permission from Sir Robert Raines to use his famous Cup horse Tristram in a trial gallop. The horse will be here to-morrow, and we can put them together with one or two more the next morning. Sir Robert is coming over to see it. He takes a great interest in her; he owns her sire King Charles."

"Sir Robert coming?" said Hector doubtfully.

"He'll never recognize you—no one would, not even——"

Picton pulled himself up short. He had spoken unthinkingly and stopped just in time; but Hector was not satisfied.

"Not even—whom did you mean?" he asked.

"Never mind; it was a slip; I forgot."

"Lenise Elroy?" asked Hector calmly.

"Yes, I thought of her."

"And you think she, even that woman, would not recognize me?"

"I am certain she would not. She might have done so when you escaped, but not now. Your illness has changed you in a very strange way. I can hardly believe you are Hector sometimes," said Picton.

"Then I must be safe," he said, smiling. "Speaking of Mrs. Elroy," he went on, "did I tell you I saw her in Torquay?"

"No," said Picton surprised. "Where? Are you sure?"

"I was passing a hotel when something prompted me to cross the road and look in at the window. I saw her seated at the supper table, laughing gayly with people, a man beside her, probably her lover, he seemed infatuated with her. She is still very beautiful, the same luring smile, and eyes like stars; you can imagine how I felt. The sight was too much for me, as I contrasted her position with mine. I raised my hands and appealed to God for justice. My prayer was answered, for a little farther on, as I staggered down the road, I came across that great-hearted fellow Brack. You know the rest."

"Yes, I know the rest," said Picton.

They were in the study and could talk freely. No one ventured in except Captain Ben, and he came at this moment. He saw something serious was going on; shutting the door quietly he sat down.

"Hector is going away, to London. He can't stand the associations at Haverton. It is not to be wondered at," said Picton.

"I'm surprised he stood it so long; I know what it must have cost him. You're brave, Hector, far braver than we are. By God, you're a man if ever there was one!" said Ben in his straight manner.

"A man can bear far more than he imagines. Torture of the mind is greater than torture of the body," said Hector.

"You're right, no doubt," said Ben. "But why London, why go there?"

"I have my reasons; they are powerful. On board the Sea-mew I laid my plans; I think I shall succeed," said Hector.

"Would you like Ben to go with you?" asked Picton.

"No—he'd be too merciful," said Hector calmly.

They looked at him; he spoke quietly, but there was that in his voice and face boded ill for somebody.

"When are you going?" asked Ben.

"After Tearaway has had her trial with Tristram," said Hector.

"That will be worth seeing," said Ben.

"And the filly will beat Sir Robert's horse," said Picton.

"I doubt it," said Ben. "Think what he's done, and Ascot Cup winner, Doncaster Cup Cesarewitch, Metropolitan, Northumberland Plate—he must be the best stayer in England."

"So he is," said Picton, "but Tearaway will beat him for speed at the finish. Blackett says he'll put them together over two miles, with only seven pounds between them. I suggested level weights but he doesn't want to take the heart out of her."

"If she can beat Tristram at seven pounds she's the best filly ever seen," said Ben.

"And I believe she is," was Picton's enthusiastic comment.

Hector Woodridge sat in his room, when everything was still in the house, and thought over his plans. No one recognized him, Picton said even Lenise Elroy would not recognize him; so much the better, for he had dealings with her.

How he hated this woman, who had fooled him to the top of his bent and done him so great an injury! She must suffer. Did she suffer now? She must, there was some sort of conscience in her. Her beauty appealed to him once; never would it do so again. She knew he was innocent, the only person who did, and he intended wringing a confession from her.

Fortunately he had money. His brother was generous, and offered him more than he had a right to expect; he would make it up to him some day, when he had completed the work he intended.

There was a man on Dartmoor, and there was Brack: they must be rewarded for their kindness, for the help they had given him. And there was that gracious lady who assisted him as he tramped to Torquay. He had not forgotten her face, it was engraven on his memory. He was thinking of her now, how she gave him the coat, the boots, food, and spoke kindly to him. When times were changed, and his work done, he would seek her out again and thank her. His heart warmed toward her; he contrasted her purity with that of the other woman, and wondered how he could have been caught in Lenise Elroy's toils.

Elroy was a weak-minded, foolish fellow; she married him for his money. He recalled his first meeting with her; they were mutually attracted, and so it went on and on, from bad to worse, until the end, when the fatal shot was fired.

And since then? He could not bear to think of it all. He vowed Lenise Elroy should pay the penalty as he had, that her tortures of mind should equal his; then she would know what he had suffered; no, not a tenth part of it; but even that would overwhelm her.

CHAPTER XV

"THE ST. LEGER'S IN YOUR POCKET"

TRISTRAM arrived at Haverton; Sir Robert Raines came the same day; everything was in readiness for the trial next morning.

Sir Robert was a great racing man, came of a sporting family, had a fine seat about forty miles from Haverton, called Beaumont Hall, where he kept a stud of horses and about thirty or forty racers. He was well known as a plunger, and had landed some big stakes; occasionally he was hard hit, but so far the balance had been on the right side. He and the Woodridges had been friends for years; he had known the Admiral and admired him. He had also known Raoul Elroy and his wife, and been present at Hector's trial, on the grand jury, and after. Sir Robert was loath to believe Hector guilty, but on the evidence could arrive at no other conclusion. The result of the trial made no difference in his friendship with the Admiral and Picton; when the former died he helped his son to the best of his ability. He had a great liking for Captain Ben, which was returned.

It was a critical moment when Hector was introduced to him as William Rolfe, "a friend of mine from Devonshire," said Picton.

Sir Robert shook hands with him; it was easy to see he had no idea it was Hector Woodridge, and all breathed more freely.

"So you imagine you've got the winner of the St. Leger at Haverton, eh, Pic?" he said as they sat smoking after dinner.

"It's more than imagination. I think Tearaway is the best filly I ever saw; so does Blackett; he says she's as fast as the wind," said Picton.

"Is she? The wind blows at a pretty pace over the wolds sometimes, sixty miles an hour or more; she's not quite up to that," said Sir Robert.

"No, not quite," laughed Picton; "but she has a rare turn of speed, and can stay as long as she's wanted."

"I haven't seen her for some time," he said.

"She's improved a lot, a real beauty; I'm sure you will say so. You ought to back her to win a good stake."

"I'm told Ripon will win. They fancy him a lot at Newmarket; they also think he had bad luck to lose the Derby."

"Suppose Tearaway beats Tristram in the morning at seven pounds difference?" said Picton.

69

"It will be the biggest certainty for the St. Leger ever known," said Sir Robert.

Hector joined in the conversation. Sir Robert liked him, but no look or word reminded him of Hector Woodridge.

"I'm safe," thought Hector. "Sir Robert ought to have been one of the first to recognize me."

Next morning they were all on the moor early. Four horses were to take part in the trial: Tristram, Tearaway, Rodney and Admiral, and the filly was giving weight to all except Sir Robert's great horse.

"By jove, she has grown into a beauty!" exclaimed the baronet when he saw the beautiful black filly with Fred Erickson, the popular Yorkshire jockey, in the saddle. Erickson lived at Haverton village, but was not often at home, as he had an enormous amount of riding, going to scale under eight stone easily.

"Good morning, Fred," said Sir Robert. "You're on a nice filly."

"She is, Sir Robert; one of the best."

"Can she beat Tristram? You've ridden him."

"I wouldn't go so far as that, but she'll give him a good race," said the jockey.

Abel Dent came from Beaumont Hall to ride Tristram in the gallop. He was always on the horse's back in his work and knew him thoroughly.

"You'll have to keep him going, Abe," said Sir Robert, smiling.

"I'll keep 'em all going," was the confident reply.

Rodney and Admiral were more than useful; the latter was to bring them along for the last mile, it was his favorite distance.

Brant Blackett greeted them as he rode up on his cob. He was brimful of confidence as to the result of the spin. He set Tearaway to give Rodney and Admiral a stone each.

"I'll send them down to the two-mile post," he said.

"This is the best long gallop anywhere, I should say," said Sir Robert. "I often envy it you, Pic, my boy. Fancy four miles straight— it's wonderful."

It was indeed a glorious sight. The moor stretched away for miles, undulating, until it was lost in the hill in the distance. The training ground had been reclaimed from it, snatched from its all-devouring grasp, and been perfected at great expense. Beside the somber brown of the wild moorland it looked a brilliant, dazzling green.

Haverton Moor harbored vast numbers of birds, and the grouse shooting was among the best in Yorkshire. Picton Woodridge owned the moor; it was not profitable, but he loved it, and would sooner have parted with fertile farms than one acre of this brown space. It was not dull this morning; the sun touched everything, and as far as the eye could see there were billows of purple, brown, green, yellow, and tinges of red. A haze hung over it when they arrived, but gradually floated away like gossamer and disappeared into space. The air was bracing; it was good to be out on such a morning, far away from the noise and bustle of the busy world; a feeling of restfulness, which nature alone gives, was over all.

To Hector, however, it recalled memories which made him shudder. He thought of that great moor he had so recently been a prisoner on, and of his escape, and the privations he suffered. There was not the cruel look about Haverton, and there was no prison in its space.

Blackett sent his head lad to start them. Looking through powerful glasses he saw when they moved off and said, "They're on the way; we shall know something."

The three were galloping straight toward them at a tremendous pace.

Rodney held the lead; he would be done with at the end of the first mile, then Admiral would jump in and pilot them home.

Abe Dent meant winning on Tristram; he had little doubt about it. How could Tearaway be expected to beat him at a difference of only seven pounds? It was absurd!

Rodney fell back, and Admiral took command with a six lengths' lead. The lad on him had instructions to come along at top speed, and was nothing loath; he knew his mount was a smasher over a mile.

Tearaway was in the rear, Erickson keeping close behind Tristram. When Admiral took Rodney's place the jockey knew the filly was going splendidly; he felt sure he could pass Tristram at any time.

Dent saw Admiral sailing ahead and went after him; the gap lessened, Tristram got within three lengths and stopped there. Sir Robert's horse was a great stayer, but he lacked the sprinting speed for a lightning finish. This was where Tearaway had the advantage.

"What a pace!" exclaimed Sir Robert. "By jove, Pic, you've got a wonder in that filly, but she'll not beat my fellow."

"They have half a mile to go yet," said the trainer. "There'll be a change before long."

So great was the pace that Admiral ran himself out at the end of six furlongs and came back to Tristram. Fred saw this, and giving Tearaway a hint she raced up alongside the Cup horse.

When Dent saw her head level with him he set to work on his mount. Tristram always finished like a bulldog, and had to be ridden out. He gained again.

Sir Robert saw it and said: "He'll come right away now."

So thought the others, with the exception of the trainer; he sat on his cob, a self-satisfied smile on his face.

"Wait till Fred turns the tap on," he thought.

Erickson was not long in doing this. He knew Tearaway's speed was something abnormal; in his opinion nothing could stand against it.

In answer to his call, Tearaway swooped down on Tristram again, drew level, headed him, left him, and was a length ahead before Dent recovered from the shock. On came Tearaway. They looked in amazement. Sir Robert could hardly believe his eyes. What a tremendous pace at the end of a two-mile gallop.

"What did I tell you!" exclaimed the trainer triumphantly. "Fast as the wind, you bet she is."

The black filly came on, increasing her lead at every stride; she passed them a good couple of lengths ahead of Tristram, Admiral toiling in the rear.

"Wonderful!" exclaimed Sir Robert. He seemed puzzled to account for it. Was Tristram off color? He must ask Dent.

The pair pulled up and came slowly to the group.

"Anything wrong with my horse?" asked Sir Robert.

"No, sir; he galloped as well as ever, but that filly's a wonder, a holy terror, never saw anything like it, she flew past him—her pace is tremendous," and Dent looked at Tearaway with a sort of awe.

"Won easily," said Fred. "Never had to press her. I had the measure of Tristram all the way; I could have raced up to him at any part of the spin. Look at her now. She doesn't blow enough to put a match out; you can't feel her breathing hardly. She's the best racer I ever put my leg across."

"Pic, the St. Leger's in your pocket," said Sir Robert, as he shook him heartily by the hand.

CHAPTER XVI

HOW HECTOR FOUGHT THE BLOODHOUND

THE night before Hector was to leave Haverton he sat with his brother and Captain Ben in the study. They had been talking over Tearaway's wonderful trial, and Picton said he should back her to win the biggest stake he had ever gone for.

"And you shall have half if she wins, as I feel sure she will," he said to Hector.

"You are too good," said Hector; "but I won't refuse it. I may want it. I have a difficult and expensive game to play."

"Don't run into danger," said Ben.

"I'll avoid it where possible," said Hector.

"You have not told us how you escaped from prison," said Picton. "Perhaps it is too painful a subject."

"Painful it is, but I fully intended telling you. I may as well do it now. I want to recompense the man on the moor, also Brack, without whose assistance I should not have boarded the Sea-mew. I protested but he insisted on taking me there. I thought my presence on board might compromise you. Brack asked me what I would do if you and I changed places and I confessed to myself I would help you to escape."

"Did you doubt what I would do?" asked Picton.

"No, but I did not wish you to run any risk for my sake."

"That was unkind; you know I would do anything for you," said Picton.

"Anyhow, I am glad Brack insisted on my going on the Sea-mew," said Hector, smiling. "I had some luck in getting away. I do not think the warders thought I would try to escape—I had been quiet and orderly during the time I had been there. When the gang I was in returned to the prison I managed to creep away and hide in some bushes. I had no irons on, I had a good deal of liberty, most of the men liked me, one or two of them were kind and pitied me. It was much easier to slip away than I anticipated. When I was alone I ran as fast as I could across the moor. They were not long in discovering I was missing, and as I fled I heard the gun fired, giving warning that a prisoner had escaped. The sound echoed across the moor; I knew every man's hand was against me but I meant making a fight for liberty. Even the hour's freedom I had enjoyed helped me. I was out of prison, alone on the moor, I determined not to be taken back—I would sooner die. I knew there were many old disused quarries, and limekilns, about. Could I not hide in one of these? No; they would be sure to search them. I must get into densely wooded country, among the bushes and undergrowth, and hide there. I was weak in body, for my health had broken down, but I kept on until nightfall, when I sank down exhausted in a mass of bracken and fell asleep. The sun was up when I awoke. I looked cautiously round, starting at every sound; a bird in the trees, or a rabbit scuttling away made me nervous. I saw no one about, so I hurried along, taking advantage of every bit of cover. I passed the back of a huge Tor, which reared its granite head high above the country, like a giant hewn in stone. It looked cold, bleak, forbidding, had a stern aspect, made me shudder; I hurried away from it across more open country. How to get rid of my clothes and obtain others puzzled me. I had no money; if it came to the worst I must watch some farm house where there was a chance of making an exchange. I dare not face any one; when I saw a man coming toward me I hid until he passed. I knew the trackers were after me, that a thorough search would be made, and the feeling that I was being hunted down almost overwhelmed me. I had nothing to eat except a few berries and roots; the nights were cold and I lay shivering, ill, and worn out. Two days passed and I began to think I had a chance. My prison clothes were the great hindrance. I could not leave the moor in them: it meant certain capture. I did not know in which direction I was traveling; my one object was to go on and on until an opportunity offered to rid myself of the tell-tale garments.

"Almost done up for want of food, and the long tramp, I sat down to rest on a rock, from which I had a good view of the moor, although I was hidden from sight. I knew telescopes and glasses would be used, and that I should be discovered if I showed myself.

"I saw no one about, but about a mile distant was a farm house. It was in a lonely, bleak spot. I wondered if the people in it were as cold as the country; they could hardly be blamed if their surroundings hardened them, made them callous to human suffering. I don't know what it was, but something prompted me to go toward this house. I walked along, keeping under cover where possible, until half the distance had been traversed.

"As I walked I fancied I heard a peculiar sound behind me. It chilled my blood in me; it made me tremble. I dare not look back, I stood still, panting with horror. It was not the sound of human footsteps, and yet something was coming after me; I distinctly heard the thud on the ground, and whatever it was it must be drawing nearer.

"I cannot convey to you any idea of the peculiar unearthly sound I heard, no description of mine could be adequate, but you can imagine something of what I felt, weak and overtaxed as I was, my mind in a whirl, my legs deadly tired and numbed, every part of my body aching. The sound came nearer. Then a noise which increased my horror—I had heard it before, near the prison—it was the bay of a hound—a bloodhound was on my track. I knew what such a brute would do, pull me down, tear me, fasten his teeth in me, worry me to death. In desperation I turned and stood still. I saw the bloodhound coming along at a fast pace, scenting the ground, then baying from time to time. He lifted his huge head and saw me. I fancied I saw fire flash in his eyes, his mouth looked blood red, his huge jaws and cheeks hung massively on each side. He was a great beast, savage, with the lust of blood on him, and he came straight at me. There was a chain attached to his collar, so I judged he must have wrenched away from the man who held him in leash. He was within fifty yards of me and I prepared to grapple with him; I had no intention of allowing my weakness to overcome me. Fight him I must. It was his life or mine; but how could I wrestle with so much brute strength in my feeble condition? He came at me with the ferocity of a lion. He leaped upon me, and I caught him by the collar. He bit and scratched my hands, but I did not let go. For a moment I held him, his savage face glared into mine, his huge paws were on my chest, he stood on his hind legs, the incarnation of brute strength. We glared at each other. Like a lightning flash it crossed my mind that I must loose my hold on the collar and grasp his throat with both hands, throttle him. This was easier thought than done, for once I loosened my grip on the collar he might wrench himself free and hurl me to the ground; then his teeth would be at my throat instead of my hands at his. I did it in a second. He almost slipped me; he was very cunning—the moment I loosened my hold on the collar he seemed to know my intention. But I had him, held him, put all my strength with it and felt his windpipe gradually being crushed closer and closer. At that moment I think I was as great a savage as the bloodhound, I felt if it had been a man I held by the throat I should have done the same to free myself. How he struggled! We fell to the ground and rolled over, but I never loosened my hold and hardly felt the pain in my hands. He tore me with his feet, scratching, striving to bite me and failing. We rolled over and over but I did not let go. I was almost exhausted when the hound's struggle relaxed—in a few minutes he was dead. No one can imagine the feeling of relief and thankfulness that came over me. I offered up a prayer for my delivery from a terrible death, then sank down in a faint by his side.

"When I came to I thought what I should do. There would be another hound on the track, I must put it off the scent. The smell of my clothes was what they were following; I knew this from what I had been told in the prison. I must get rid of the clothes. I stripped them off and laid them on the bloodhound, then I tied my coarse vest round my loins and started toward the farm house. As I went I saw a man come out at the gate with a gun. I determined to face him, risk it, throw myself on his mercy. He saw me and stood still, staring in amazement—and well he might. At first I think he thought I was mad.

"I sank down at his feet, utterly overcome, and I saw a look of pity in his somewhat stern face and eyes.

"'You are an escaped convict,' he said.

"I acknowledged it and pleaded my innocence.

"He smiled as he said: 'They are always innocent.'

"I asked him to come and see what I had done.

"'Here, put this coat on,' he said.

"He wore a long coat, almost to his heels, and it covered me. We walked to where the hound lay. I explained what had happened, that I had wrestled with the brute and after a long struggle throttled him. He was amazed and said I was a good plucked 'un. There was no one in the house but himself, he said; the others had gone to Torquay; would I come with him and tell my story? I went, and made such an impression upon him that he said he believed my tale and would help me. He gave me some old clothes, food and drink, then hurried me on my way. He advised me to go to Torquay and try and communicate with some friends. He promised to put the searchers off the scent if they made inquiries. I said he would reap a reward for what he had done, but he did not seem to care about this. He urged me to get off the moor as quickly as possible.

"Before I left he filled my pockets with cheese, meat, and bread, and gave me an old cap, and worn-out boots. I said I should never forget him; he answered that he hoped he had done right in helping me.

"I tramped to Torquay, I—" he hesitated. No, he would not tell them of the gracious lady who assisted him and treated him as a man, not a tramp.

"I found Brack. He took me to his home, concealed me there until he contrived to smuggle me on board the Sea-mew," said Hector, as he finished his story.

"What an awful experience!" exclaimed Ben.

"Terrible!" said Picton with a shudder.

"Can you wonder that I hunger for revenge?" said Hector; and they understood him.

CHAPTER XVII

AN INTRODUCTION AT HURST PARK

IT was pure chance that led to the introduction of Hector Woodridge, as William Rolfe, to Fletcher Denyer.

Hector had been in London a week; he visited various places of amusement, showed himself openly, made no attempt at concealment. He went to the races at Hurst Park and Gatwick. It was at the famous course on the banks of the Thames that he was made known to Denyer, by a man he became friendly with at his hotel. There is much freedom on the racecourse, and men, often unknown to each other, speak on various topics connected with the sport, without introduction.

Denyer and Hector were soon in conversation, discussing the merits of various horses. Denyer received a word from the man who introduced them that Mr. Rolfe had money and might be exploited profitably to both. A hint such as this was not likely to be neglected; he thought if he could put this newly made acquaintance on a winner it would probably result in future business. He had been advised to back Frisky in the Flying Handicap, and told Hector it was a real good thing, and likely to start at a long price.

Hector wondered why he should tell him. As he looked at Denyer he fancied he had seen him before, but where he could not for the moment recall. Denyer walked away to speak to a jockey, and Hector stood trying to remember where he had met him. It flashed across his mind so vividly and suddenly that he was startled— Denyer was the man he had seen at the supper table in the hotel with Lenise Elroy. There was no doubt about it; he remembered his face distinctly. Here was a stroke of luck. Some guiding hand had led him to this man. He must cultivate his acquaintance; through him he could be brought face to face with the woman who had ruined him.

Frisky won comfortably, started at ten to one, and Hector landed a hundred pounds. He also backed the winner of the next race, the Welter Handicap, and doubled his hundred. This was encouraging; it was to be a day of success—at least it appeared so.

Denyer he did not see for some time. Shortly before the last race he noticed him walking across the paddock with a lady. It was Mrs. Elroy, and Hector's heart almost stopped beating. For a moment he trembled with nervous excitement, which by a great effort he suppressed.

They came up; Denyer introduced her. She held out her hand, Hector took it, they looked into each other's eyes. There was not a shadow of recognition on her part, but there was something else there—Lenise Elroy had by some strange intuition thrilled at the sight of this man, felt a wave of emotion flow through her body. She was sure she would like him, like him very much indeed, and she immediately resolved to better the acquaintance. Hector divined something of what passed in her mind and smiled. He could have wished for nothing better; it was what he most desired, but had not dared to hope for.

Denyer left them together for a moment.

"You are a friend of Mr. Denyer's?" she said in a soothing voice.

"I was introduced to him here," he said. "I have not known him more than an hour or so. He put me on a winner, Frisky, and I also backed the last winner. My luck is in to-day," he added, as he looked meaningly at her.

Lenise Elroy returned his glance; she understood men. She thought she had made a conquest and that he was worth it.

"Will you ride back to town with us in my motor?" said Denyer, as he joined them again.

"Yes, do, Mr. Rolfe; we shall be delighted if you will. And perhaps you will dine with us at the Savoy," she said.

Hector said he would be delighted. Fortune was indeed favoring him.

They rode to town together, and dined at the Savoy; later on they went to the Empire. It was an eventful day and night for Hector. Before he left, Denyer was half inclined to regret introducing him to Lenise; he did not care for her to show preference for another man; where she was concerned he was jealous. He reflected, however, that if she and Rolfe became good friends it would facilitate the process of extracting money from him, and this was his intention; every rich man he regarded as his lawful prey. To him Rolfe appeared rather a simple-minded, easy-going fellow; probably he had traveled a good deal, he looked tanned with the sun, as though he had been in hot climates; such men were generally free with their money, fond of company, and the society of an attractive woman like Lenise, who had very few scruples about the proprieties.

When he left, Hector promised to lunch with them the following day.

Fletcher Denyer went home with Lenise. Her maid was accustomed to seeing him in her rooms at all hours; she had never known him remain in the house for the night; she judged, and rightly, there was nothing improper in their relations. The fact of the matter was, they were mutually useful to each other. Lenise wanted some one to go about with; and Denyer not only liked her society, but found her help to him in many of his schemes.

She took off her cloak, handing it to her maid, then sat down on the couch and made herself comfortable, and attractive; she knew the full value of her personal appearance, and fine figure, and posed accordingly. Fletcher Denyer always admired her; to-night she looked so radiant and alluring he was fascinated, under her spell. He forgot his caution so far as to come to the sofa, bend over her, attempt to kiss her. She pushed him back roughly, and said: "Keep your distance, Fletcher, or we shall fall out. You have had too much champagne."

"It's not the champagne," he said hotly; "it's your beauty; it acts like wine. You are lovelier than ever to-night. That fellow Rolfe admired you, any one could see it. You're not going to throw me over for him, are you, Len?"

"Don't be a silly boy. As for throwing you over, there is no engagement between us; we are merely good friends, and if you wish to maintain the relationship you had better not try to kiss me again. I hate being kissed; kisses are only for babes and sucklings," she said.

He laughed; it was no good quarreling with her. He was satisfied to think that had any other man attempted to kiss her she would have ordered him out of the house.

"Not much of the babe about you," he said.

"More than you think, but I'm not made to be kissed."

"That's just what you are, the most lovable woman I ever met."

She laughed.

"That champagne was certainly too strong for you," she said.

She never seemed tired; all go, no matter how late the hour; her flow of spirits seldom flagged, her eyes always shone brightly, her complexion never failed her; she was really a remarkable woman. No one knew what an effort it cost her to keep up appearances—alone a change came over her, the reaction set in. She did not care to be alone, at times she was afraid.

"What do you think of Rolfe?" he asked.

"In what way?"

"All ways, as far as you can judge from what you have seen to-day, and to-night," he said.

She was thoughtful. He watched her; the jealous feeling came uppermost again.

"I think," she said slowly, "he is a man who has had a great deal of trouble, suffered much, probably on account of a woman. I think he is a strong man, that he is determined, and if he has an object in view he will attain it, no matter what the obstacles in his way. Probably he has traveled, seen a good deal of the world, had strange experiences. He has remarkable eyes, they pierce, probe into one, search out things. He is a fine looking man, well built, but has probably had a severe illness not long ago. I think I shall like him; he is worth cultivating, making a friend of."

She spoke as though no one were present. Fletcher Denyer felt for the time being he was forgotten and resented it.

"You have analyzed him closely; you must be a character reader. Have you ever turned your battery of close observation on me?" he asked snappishly.

She smiled.

"You angry man, you asked me what I think of him and I have told you. I have turned the battery on you, Fletcher. I know your worth exactly. I am useful to you; you are useful to me—that is all."

"All!" he exclaimed.

"Well, what else? We are not in love, are we?"

"No, I suppose not. Has it ever occurred to you, Lenise, that I want you to be my wife?" he asked.

"No, it has not occurred to me, nor has it occurred to you before to-night," she said.

"Yes, it has."

"I doubt it. Besides, things are much better as they are. I would not be your wife if you asked me," she said.

"Why not?" he asked.

"Because—oh, for the very sufficient reason that you could not keep me, and I have sufficient to live upon," she said.

He saw it would be better to drop the subject and said: "You have no objection to giving me a helping hand?"

"In what way?"

"This man Rolfe has money. I don't agree with your estimate of him as a strong man; I think he is weak. He may be useful to me."

"You mean he may be induced to finance some of your schemes?" she said.

"Yes; why not? Where's the harm? His money is as good as another's, or better."

"And you think I will lure him into your financial net?" she said calmly.

80

"Not exactly that; you can hint that I sometimes get in the know, behind the scenes, and so on, then leave the rest to me," he said.

"Take care, Fletcher. This man Rolfe is more than your equal; I am sure of it. If he is drawn into your schemes it will be for some object of his own. Don't drag me into it."

"There's no dragging about it. You have merely to give me a good character, say I am clever and shrewd—you know how to work it," he said.

"Yes, I think I know how to work it," she said quietly.

CHAPTER XVIII

CONSCIENCE TROUBLES

LENISE ELROY sat in her bedroom long after Fletcher Denyer left the house. She dismissed her maid before undressing, who, accustomed to her mistress's moods, thought nothing of it.

"I hate being alone," she said to herself, "and yet it is only then I can throw off the mask. I am a wicked woman; at least I have been told so, long ago. Perhaps I am, or was at that time. I wonder if Hector Woodridge is dead, or if he escaped? It is hardly likely he got away. I could wish he had, if he were out of the country and I were safe. It was not my fault altogether; he has suffered, so have I, and suffer still. I loved him in those days, whatever he may have thought to the contrary, but I don't think he loved me. Had Raoul been a man it would never have happened, but he was a weak, feeble-minded mortal and bored me intensely. I ought not to have married him; it was folly—money is not everything. I could have been a happy woman with such a man as Hector. How he must have suffered! But so have I. There is such a thing as conscience; I discovered it long ago, and it has tormented me, made my life at times a hell. I have tried to stifle it and cannot. Ever since that night at Torquay I have been haunted by a horrible dread that he got away on his brother's yacht, the Sea-mew. Captain Bruce is devoted to them, he would do anything to help them. Perhaps it was part of the plan that the Sea-mew should lie in Torbay waiting for his escape. Money will do a great deal, and bribery may have been at work. It seems hardly possible, but there is no telling. The boatman said he was dead, Hackler said the same; they may be wrong—who knows—and at this moment he may be free and plotting against me. I can expect no mercy from him; I have wronged him too deeply; it is not in human nature to forgive what I have done."

She shuddered, her face was drawn and haggard, she looked ten years older than she did an hour ago.

"Do I regret what happened?" she asked herself. She could not honestly say she did; given the same situation over again she felt everything would happen as it did then. It was a blunder, a crime, and the consequences were terrible, but it freed her, she was left to live her life as she wished, and it was an intense relief to be rid of Raoul. She knew it was callous, wicked, to think like this, but she could not help it. She had not been a bad woman since her husband's death, not as bad women go. She had had one or two love affairs, but she had been circumspect, there was no more scandal, and she did no harm. She prided herself on this, as she thought of the opportunities and temptations that were thrown in her way and had been resisted.

"I'm not naturally a bad woman," she reasoned. "I do not lure men to destruction, fleece them of their money, then cast them aside. I have been merciful to young fellows who have become infatuated with me, chilled their ardor, made them cool toward me, saved them from themselves." She recalled two or three instances where she had done this and it gave her satisfaction.

Her conscience, however, troubled her, and never more than to-night. She could not account for it. Why on this particular night should she be so vilely tormented? It was no use going to bed; she could not sleep; at least not without a drug, and she had taken too many of late. Sleep under such circumstances failed to soothe her; she awoke with a heavy head and tired eyes, her body hardly rested.

She got up and walked to and fro in the room. She was debating what to do, how to act. Never since her love affair with Hector Woodridge had she met a man who appealed to her as William Rolfe did. The moment she was introduced to him at the races she knew he was bound to influence her life for good, or evil. She recognized the strong man in him, the man who could bend her to his will; she knew in his hands she would be as weak as the weakest of her sex, that she would yield to him. More, she wished him to dominate her, to place herself in his power, to say to him, "I am yours; do what you will with me." All this swept over her as she looked into his eyes and caught, she fancied, an answering response. She had felt much of this with Hector Woodridge, but not all; William Rolfe had a surer hold of her, if he wished to exercise his power, she knew it.

Did she wish him to exercise the power?

She thought no, and meant yes. Fletcher Denyer was useful to her, but in her heart she despised him; he took her money without scruple when she offered it. She was quite certain Rolfe would not do so, even if he wanted it ever so badly. She had no fear of Denyer, or his jealous moods. She smiled as she thought of him in his fits of anger, spluttering like a big child. Rolfe was a man in every respect, so she thought; she was a woman who liked to be subdued by a strong hand. The tragedy in her life had not killed her love of pleasure, although the result of it, as regards Hector Woodridge, had caused her much pain. Still she was a woman who cast aside trouble and steeled herself against it. She had not met a man who could make her forget the past and live only in the present, but now she believed William Rolfe could do it.

Would he try, would he come to her? She thought it possible, probable; and if he did, how would she act? Would she confess what had happened in her life? She must, it would be necessary, there would be no deception with such a man. What would be the consequences—would he pity, or blame her?

At last she went to bed, and toward morning fell asleep, a restless slumber, accompanied by unpleasant dreams. It was eleven o'clock when she dressed; she remembered she had to meet Fletcher and William Rolfe at luncheon. She took a taxi to the hotel, and found Rolfe waiting for her. He handed her a note; it was from Denyer, stating he was detained in the city on urgent business, apologizing for his unavoidable absence, asking Rolfe to meet him later on, naming the place.

He watched her as she read it, and saw she was pleased; it gave him savage satisfaction. He had not thought his task would be so easy; everything worked toward the end he had in view.

"I hope you will keep your appointment, at any rate," he said.

"I have done so, I am here," she answered, smiling.

"I mean that you will lunch with me."

"Would it be quite proper?" she asked with a challenging glance.

"Quite," he said. "I will take every care of you."

She wondered how old he was. It was difficult to guess. He might be younger than herself—not more than a year or two at the most. What caused that look on his face? It certainly was not fear; he was fearless, she thought. It was a sort of hunted look, as though he were always expecting something to happen and was on his guard. She would like to know the cause of it.

"You cannot imagine how difficult I am to take care of," she said.

"I am not afraid of the task," he said. "Will you lunch with me?"

"With pleasure," she replied, and they went inside.

The room was well filled, a fashionable crowd; several people knew Mrs. Elroy and acknowledged her. To a certain extent she had lived down the past, but the recollection of it made her the more interesting. Women were afraid of her attractions, especially those who had somewhat fickle husbands; their alarm was groundless, had they known it.

"Wonder who that is with her? He's a fine looking man, but there's something peculiar about him," said a lady.

"What do you see peculiar in him? Seems an ordinary individual to me," drawled her husband.

"He is not ordinary by any means; his complexion is peculiar, a curious yellowy brown," she said.

"Perhaps he's a West Indian, or something of that sort."

They sat at a small table alone; she thoroughly enjoyed the lunch. She drank a couple of glasses of champagne and the sparkling wine revived her.

"Shall we go for a motor ride after?" he asked.

"Yes, if you wish, and will not be tired of my company," she said.

"You do yourself an injustice," he said. "I do not think you could tire any one."

She laughed as she said: "You don't know much of me, I am dull at times, rather depressed." She sighed, and for a moment the haggard look came into her face. Hector wondered if remorse were accountable for it; if she ever repented the injury she had done; no, it was not possible or she would have stretched out her hand to save him. He steeled his heart against her; he hated her; he would have his revenge, cost her what it might.

They entered a taxi and were driven in the direction of Staines and Windsor. She felt a strange thrill of pleasure as she sat close beside him.

CHAPTER XIX

"WHAT WOULD YOU DO?"

THEY went along the Staines Road, then by the banks of the Thames past Runnymede, came to Old Windsor, and from there to the White Hart Hotel. She thoroughly enjoyed it; the drive nerved her; she forgot the painful reflections of the previous night. He talked freely. She noticed with satisfaction he seemed attracted by her, looked at her searchingly as though interested. They went on the river and were rowed past the racecourse. It was warm and fine, the flow of the water past the boat soothed her. They had tea at the hotel, then returned to town.

"Where to?" he asked when they were nearing Kensington. She gave the name of her flat and they alighted there.

"I have been here some time," she said. "I find it comfortable and quiet. Will you come in?"

He followed her. He noticed her room was furnished expensively and in excellent taste; there was nothing grand or gaudy about it.

"I am alone here, with my maid," she said. "They have an excellent system: all meals are prepared downstairs and sent up; there is a very good chef."

"The least possible trouble," he said. "How long have you been here?"

"Three years. It suits me; I do not care to be away from London. In my married days I lived in the country, but it bored me to death. Do you like the country?"

"Yes, I love it; but then much of my life has been spent in solitude."

"You have traveled?"

"Yes."

"I thought so."

"Why?"

"Your complexion denotes it. I like it, there is a healthy brown about it."

"I have done much hard work in my time," he said.

"Mining?" she asked.

"Yes, I suppose you would call it that."

"Where?"

"On Dartmoor," he said.

She was so astonished she could not speak. She looked at him with fear in her eyes.

"Dartmoor?" she whispered. "I did not know there were mines on Dartmoor."

"Oh, yes, there are—copper mines. I was fool enough to believe there was money in them, but I was mistaken; there is copper there, no doubt, but I did not find it," he said.

She felt as though a snake fascinated her, that she must ask questions about it.

"I have been to Torquay, but I did not go to Dartmoor," she said.

"You ought to have done so; it is a wonderful place. I was there a long time. When were you in Torquay?"

She told him.

"Strange," he said; "I was there at that time."

She felt a curious dread, not of him, but of something unknown.

"I went to the races—a friend of mine was riding there. He won four events. Lucky, was it not?"

"Yes," she said faintly. "Who was he?"

"Picton Woodridge. His yacht the Sea-mew was in the bay. I was on it."

"You!" she exclaimed, and he saw the fear in her eyes.

"Yes, why not? Is there anything strange about it?" he asked, smiling. "He lives at Haverton. He is rich, but he is not quite happy."

"Why not, if he has everything he wants?"

"He has not everything he wants; no one has, as a matter of fact. It would not be good for us. You have not all you want."

"No, I have not; but I get along very well."

"What is missing out of your life?" he asked.

"I can hardly tell you."

"My friend's life is overcast by a great calamity that befell his family some years ago."

"What was it?" she asked, and a slight shiver passed through her.

"His brother was accused of murder, of shooting the husband of the woman he had fallen in love with. He was condemned and reprieved; he is at Dartmoor now. That is enough to make his brother's life unhappy; it killed the Admiral, their father."

"How shocking!" she said.

"I never thought of it before, but, strange to say, the man's name was Elroy. It is your name," he said.

She laughed uneasily; she could not tell him now.

87

"I hope you do not connect me with the lady in question?"

"No, of course not. How absurd! But still it is strange—the name is uncommon," he said.

"I suppose you never saw his brother at the prison?"

"I did—I wish I had not."

"Did he look very ill, broken down?"

"He was a terrible wreck. He suffered awful agony, of mind more than body. I never saw such a change in a man in my life. When I knew Hector Woodridge he was a fine, well set up, handsome man, in the army, a soldier's career before him. The breakdown was complete; it made me suffer to look at him. I never went again and I do not think he wanted it. If ever a man was living in hell upon earth he was; the wonder is it did not kill him."

"How terrible!" she said.

"I wonder if the woman suffers? He did it on her account. I do not believe he is guilty—I am certain he is not. His brother believes in his innocence, so does Captain Bruce, and all his friends. I believe it is the knowledge that he is innocent sustains him in his awful life; he told me he hoped one day to prove his innocence, but that his lips were sealed, he could not speak. I told him that was foolish, that it was due to himself to speak, but he shook his head and said, 'Impossible!'"

"Is it a very terrible place at Dartmoor?"

"I suppose it is like all such prisons; but think what it must be for an innocent man to be caged there with a lot of desperate criminals, the scum of the earth. What must it be for such a man as Hector Woodridge, cultured, refined, an army man, well-bred—and on the top of it all the knowledge that the disgrace killed his father. It would drive me mad."

"And me too," she said. "You say he is there still?"

"Yes; there is no chance of his escaping. I wish he could."

"A prisoner escaped when I was at Torquay. I saw it in the local paper," she said.

"So did I; the fellow had a terrible fight with a bloodhound and strangled it. A desperate man has desperate strength," he said.

"I met an old boatman named Brack there; he told me the man must be dead."

"No doubt; fell down a disused mine, or drowned himself, poor devil. I don't wonder at it," he said.

"I wonder how the woman feels about it?" she said in a low voice. "She must suffer, her conscience must trouble her, in a way her life must be as hard to bear as his."

"That depends on the woman," he said. "I believe she can prove his innocence; something tells me she can; his brother

88

believes it too. If this be so, she ought to speak and save him, no matter at what cost to herself."

"Do you think she will?"

"No; or she would have spoken before. She must be callous, hard-hearted, dead to all sense of human feeling. Such a woman would make me shudder to come in contact with her," he said.

She smiled as she thought: "He little knows I am that woman. I must wait. If he loves me later on I can tell him."

"Perhaps the woman cannot prove his innocence. She may believe him guilty."

"Impossible. There were only three persons present: the husband, the wife, and Hector Woodridge."

"It seems very strange that if he is innocent she has not declared the truth."

"Steeped in wickedness and sin as she is, I do not wonder at it; she is probably living in the world, leading a fast life, ruining men as she ruined him."

"Or she may be suffering agonies and be too much of a coward to speak; she may be an object of pity; perhaps if you saw her you would be sorry for her, as sorry as you are for him," she said.

"He is in prison, she is free; she has the world to distract her, he has nothing."

"You spoke of torture of the mind. Perhaps she is a sensitive woman; if so, her sufferings are as terrible as his."

"If you were the woman, what would you do?" he asked.

The question was put with an abruptness that startled her; again a feeling of fear was uppermost. It was strange he should know Hector Woodridge; still more curious that he was on the Sea-mew in Torbay. He must know if Hector Woodridge boarded the yacht; was he concealing something?

"I do not know what I should do. It would depend upon circumstances."

"What circumstances?" he asked.

"If I knew he was innocent, I should speak, I think—that is, if I could prove it."

"She must be able to prove it," he said. "I believe he is suffering, keeping silent, to save her."

"If he is, his conduct is heroic," she said.

"Foolish—a sin and a shame that he should waste his life for such a woman."

"You think her a very bad woman?"

"I do, one of the worst," he said.

She sighed.

"I am glad I have never been placed in such an unfortunate position," she said.

"So am I, but I am sure if you had been, Hector Woodridge would be a free man," he said.

"I wonder if he loved her?" she asked quickly.

"Loved her? He must have done so. Think how he is suffering for her; he must love her still," he said.

"Perhaps she does not know this."

"She ought to know; all his actions speak of love for her. No man ever made a greater sacrifice for a woman," he said. Then, looking at his watch, he added, "It is time for me to go, to meet Mr. Denyer. He is a great friend of yours, is he not?"

"I should not call him a friend exactly, although I have known him a long time; he is useful to me in business matters," she said.

"Can I be of any use in that way?" he asked.

"You might; I will ask you if I require anything."

"And then I shall be an acquaintance," he said, smiling.

"Would you rather be my friend?"

"Yes."

She held out her hand.

"I do not think that will be difficult," she said, her eyes flashing into his.

CHAPTER XX

RITA SEES A RESEMBLANCE

SOME acquaintanceships ripen fast into friendship; it was so with Lenise Elroy and Hector, at least on her side. She knew him as William Rolfe and as such he appealed to her. At times he reminded her in a vague way of Hector Woodridge; she liked him none the worse for this, although it brought back painful memories. She was fast drifting into the ocean of love where she would be tossed about, buffeted by the waves, and probably damaged. The impression he made on her was not easily effaced; she began to neglect Fletcher Denyer, much to his mortification. Before she met Rolfe their connection had been smooth, going on the even tenor of its way, with nothing to mar the harmony, but this new acquaintance proved a disturbing element and she was no longer the same to him. He resented it but could do nothing; he was powerless. He spoke to her, remonstrated, and she laughed at him; it was of no use tackling Rolfe, who would probably tell him to mind his business.

He had, however, no intention of relinquishing what little hold he had over her, and tried to make himself more indispensable. Rolfe was friendly, took a hint as to some speculative shares and made money.

It was September and the St. Leger day drew near. Hector had not forgotten Tearaway. He did not write to his brother; he thought it better not, safer. He watched the papers and saw the filly occasionally quoted at a hundred to four taken. The secret of the trial had been well kept, nothing leaked out about it. Ripon was a firm favorite at three to one, and all the wise men at Newmarket were sanguine of his success. Bronze was much fancied in certain quarters, and Harriet, The Monk, and Field Gun, frequently figured in the list; there was every prospect of a larger field than usual.

Fletcher Denyer often talked about racing with Hector, who was quite willing to discuss the chances of horses with him.

"I am told on the best authority Bronze will win," said Fletcher. "What do you fancy, Rolfe?"

"I haven't thought much about it," replied Hector. "If Bronze is as good as they make out, he must have a chance."

"If you want to back him I can get your money on at a good price," said Fletcher.

"I'll think it over," said Hector.

Mrs. Elroy was also interested in the St. Leger. She knew the owner of Ripon, who told her he did not think his horse had anything to fear. This news was imparted to Hector.

"Are you going to Doncaster?" she asked.

He said he was, that he always liked to see the St. Leger run.

"I think I shall go," she said. "I have been asked to join a house party near Doncaster."

Hector wondered how it came about that a woman who had behaved so badly could be so soon forgiven, and her past forgotten.

"Then I shall have the pleasure of seeing you there," he said.

"I hope so. Your friend Mr. Woodridge has something in the race—Tearaway, is it not? I suppose she hasn't got much of a chance, it is such a good price about her," she said.

"No, I don't expect she has or she would not be at such long odds," he answered.

"There have been some big surprises in the St. Leger," she said.

"It doesn't look like one this year," he replied.

A few days before the Doncaster meeting, Hector went to Haverton, where he had a warm welcome. Sir Robert Raines was there, Captain Ben, and one or two more, including Dick Langford, and Rita. Lady Raines came to act as hostess for Picton and brought two of her daughters; it was the knowledge that she would be there induced Rita to come with her brother.

At first Picton hesitated to ask her; she had never been to Haverton; but finally he decided. Lady Raines and her daughters would be there, it would be all right and proper. He was delighted when he heard she had arranged to come with Dick.

Hector came the following day after their arrival. He first saw Rita in the garden with Picton. He recognized her at once: it was the lady who had been so kind to him on his way from Dartmoor to Torquay. He saw how close they walked together, how confidential was their talk, and guessed the rest. He recognized this with a pang; he had built castles in the air about her, which, like most such edifices, are easily shattered. Would she know him again as the tramp she helped on the road? It was not likely. In the first place, he was greatly changed, and secondly she would never expect to find him here. He smiled grimly as he thought of the condition he was in the last time they met. He went out to face her and walked toward them.

Picton introduced them. She started slightly as she looked at him.

"I thought I had seen you somewhere before," she said with a bright smile. "You quite startled me, but I dare not tell you about it, it is quite too ridiculous."

"You have roused my curiosity. Please enlighten me," he said.

"You are quite sure you will not be offended?" She looked at them both.

"I shall not, and I am the principal person to consider," said Hector.

"Then, if you promise not to be angry with me, I will; after all, I am sure he was a gentleman although in reduced circumstances," she said.

"Who was a gentleman?" asked Picton.

"The man I for the moment fancied resembled Mr. Rolfe," she said. "It was the day you came to Torwood."

Rita told them about the tramp she had befriended, and added:

"He was a well-bred man who must have met with some great misfortune. I pitied him, my heart bled for him; he was no common man, it was easy to recognize that. He thanked me courteously and went on his way down the road. I have often thought of him since and wondered what became of him. When you first came up, Mr. Rolfe, you reminded me of him, in looks and build, that is all. Have I offended you?"

"Not at all," said Hector. "You are quite sure I am not your gentleman tramp? Look again."

"Don't be absurd! Of course you are not the man; it was a mere passing resemblance," she said.

"You did a very kindly action, and I am sure the man, whoever he is, will never forget it, or you. Perhaps at some future time he may repay your kindness. Who knows? There are some strange chances in the world, so many ups and downs, I should not at all wonder if you met him again in a very different sphere," said Hector.

Lady Raines and her daughters came on to the terrace and Rita joined them.

"Whew!" said Hector, "that was a narrow squeak, Pic. I went hot and cold all over when I recognized who it was with you, but I thought I had better come out and face the music."

"That's about the closest shave you've had, but even had she been certain she would only have known you as William Rolfe."

"I forgot that," said Hector. "Still, it is better as it is. I say, Pic, is she the one?"

"I hope so," his brother replied, laughing. "I mean to have a good try."

"Lucky fellow!" said Hector with a sigh. "There's no such chance of happiness for me."

"There may be some day," said Picton. "You have not told me what you have been doing in London."

"Plotting," said Hector. "I am on the way to secure my revenge—I shall succeed."

"Can't you give me some idea how you mean to be revenged?" asked Picton.

"Not at present. You may get an inkling at Doncaster, if you keep your eyes open; but I expect all your attention will be riveted on Tearaway," said Hector.

"That's highly probable. One doesn't own a Leger winner every year," said Picton.

"Then you think she is sure to win?"

"Certain, and Sir Robert won't hear of her defeat. He has backed her to win a large stake, and he's jubilant about it."

"It seems strange she does not shorten in the betting," said Hector.

"I don't take much notice of that; she's not a public performer, and it is a field above the average. If it had leaked out about the trial it would have been different, but we have a good lot of lads at Haverton; they know how to hold their tongues," said Picton.

"I'll tell you what, Pic, I'd like to let old Brack know. Wouldn't the dear old boy rejoice at getting on a twenty-five to one chance; he'd think more of it than anything. Brackish, boatman, Torquay, would find him," said Hector.

"He shall know," said Picton. "I'll tell you what, it would be a joke to get him to Doncaster for the St. Leger. I'll send Rose down to hunt him up and bring him."

"I'm afraid Rose would look askance at Brack, he's such a highly superior person," said Hector.

"I fancy Brack would break his reserve down before they reached Doncaster," said Picton. "I shall send him, anyway."

CHAPTER XXI

BRACK TURNS TRAVELER

ROSE, I am about to send you on an important mission to Torquay," said Picton.

"Yes, sir."

"You are to find an old boatman named Brackish, generally called Brack. He is a well-known character; there will be no difficulty about it. You will hand him this letter, and if he requires persuading you will use all your eloquence in that direction. You will give him ten pounds and pay all his expenses, and you must land him in the paddock at Doncaster at the latest on the St. Leger day. You understand?"

"Yes, sir. May I ask what kind of an individual he is?"

"Rough and ready. He was formerly a boatman at Scarborough. He is a Yorkshireman. He will don his best clothes; perhaps he will require a new pilot coat—if he does, buy him one."

"And what am I to do when I land him in the paddock, sir?"

"Wait until I see him."

"Very good, sir. Is that all?"

"Yes, I think so. Look after him well; he once did me a good turn. You'll find him interesting, also amusing."

"When shall I go, sir?"

"To-morrow; that will give you ample time—a day or two in Torquay will be a pleasant change."

"Thank you, sir; it will," said Rose.

"Come to me in my study to-night and I will give you the money," said Picton.

Robert Rose thought, as he watched him walk away: "I hope he doesn't expect me to make a friend of the man. No doubt he'll smell of the sea, and fish, tar, oil-skins, and other beastly things; it won't be a pleasant journey—we shall have to put the windows down. I wonder if he washes, or whether he's caked with dirt, like some of 'em I've seen. It's coming to a pretty pass when I am dispatched on such an errand."

He complained to Mrs. Yeoman but got no sympathy.

"If Brack's good enough for your master he's good enough for you," she snapped, and he thought it advisable not to pursue the subject farther.

Rose arrived in Torquay in due course, late at night, after a tiring journey. Next morning he went forth in quest of Brack. A policeman pointed the boatman out to him. Brack was leaning against the iron rail protecting the inner harbor. Rose looked at him in disgust. Brack had met a friend the night before and they had indulged somewhat freely in ale. He was all right but looked rather seedy and unkempt.

Rose walked up to him, putting on his best air. Brack saw him and summed him up at once.

"Somebody's flunkey," he thought.

"Are you Mr. Brackish?" asked Rose in a patronizing manner.

"I'm Brack, name Brackish, don't know about the mister, seldom hear it used when I'm addressed. Now who may you be, my good man?" said Brack, mischief lurking in his eyes.

To be addressed by this clod of a boatman as "my good man" quite upset Rose's dignity. He put on a severe look, which did not abash Brack in the least, and said: "I am from Haverton in Yorkshire. I represent Mr. Picton Woodridge. He desired me to see you and deliver this letter," and he handed it to him.

Brack took it, opened the envelope, and handed it back.

"I've lost my glasses," he said; "must have left them in 'The Sailor's Rest' last night. Me an' a mate had a few pints more than we oughter. Why the deuce didn't he post the letter and save you the trouble of comin' to see me?"

"It suited Mr. Woodridge's purpose better that I should personally deliver it. I will read it to you if you wish."

"That's what I gave it to you for," said Brack.

Rose read the letter. It was written in a kind and friendly way; Robert thought it too familiar. Brack listened attentively; at first he hardly grasped the full meaning.

"Would you mind reading it again?" he asked.

Rose did so with ill-concealed impatience; then said: "Now do you understand its import, or shall I explain more fully?"

"Don't trouble yourself. I wouldn't trouble such an almighty high personage as yourself for the world," said Brack.

"No trouble at all, I assure you," said Rose.

"As far as I understand," said Brack, "I'm to put myself in your charge and you are to convey me safely to Doncaster to see the Leger run for."

"That's it; we will leave to-morrow," said Rose.

"Will we? Who said I was goin'?" asked Brack.

"Of course you'll go; Mr. Picton wishes it."

"He ain't my master, just you remember. Brack's got no master. I'm my own boss, and a pretty stiff job I have with myself at times. Last night, for instance. As boss I ordered myself home at ten; as Brack I went on strike and declined to move—see?"

"But he will be very much disappointed if you don't go to Doncaster with me. All your expenses will be paid. You'll have ten pounds to invest on the course, and you'll back Tearaway, say at twenty to one to a fiver," said Rose.

"Shall I indeed? And pray who says Tearaway will win the Leger?"

"I do," said Rose confidently.

"And I suppose that settles it. If you say so, she must win."

"Mr. Picton says she will; so does Sir Robert Raines."

"Do they now? And I'm to take all this for gospel?"

"It's quite correct. They have all backed Tearaway to win large sums, thousands of pounds," said Rose.

"Well, it's worth considering," said Brack. He wondered if Hector Woodridge were at Haverton. It was not mentioned in the letter. Perhaps this man did not know him; he would keep quiet about it.

"You'll have to make up your mind quick because we must leave early in the morning. I was instructed to buy you a new coat, or any other thing you wanted."

"That's handsome; I'll accept the coat, a blue pilot, and a pair of boots, a tie, and a cap. I've got a fancy waistcoat my father used to wear. It's all over flowers and it's got pearl buttons. It's a knock-out; you'll admire it—perhaps you'd like to borrow it," said Brack.

Rose declined, said he would not deprive Brack of it for worlds.

"You'll come with me?" he asked.

"Oh, yes; I'll come to oblige Mr. Woodridge; he's a gent and no mistake. Will you come and see my old mother?"

Rose thought it would be diplomatic to do so. Evidently Brack was a man who wanted humoring; it was humiliating, but he must go through with it.

Old Mrs. Brackish welcomed the visitor, dusted a chair for him, treated him with apparent deference which soothed Rose's feelings. He declined to remain for dinner, making as an excuse that he never ate anything until evening, it did not agree with him, the mid-day meal. When he left it was with a sense of relief.

"The mother is better than the son," he thought; "she knew what was due to my position."

"He's a pompous old fool," she said to Brack when he was out of the house.

Brack laughed as he said: "You've hit it, mother; you generally do."

"An' so you're agoin' to Yorkshire," she said with a sigh. "Sometimes I wish I were back there, but it wouldn't suit me, and he's been very good to us here, Brack."

"We've nowt to grumble at," said Brack. "We're better off than lots o' people. I may make a bit o' money at Doncaster on Leger day—you know how lucky I am over the race."

"You oughtn't to bet," she said.

"I don't. My bit isn't bettin'; I just put a shillin' on now and again for the fun of the thing. Where's the harm in that?" he asked.

"I suppose you know best, Brack, and you've always been a good son to me," she said.

"And I always shall, have no fear of that, mother." And she had not; her faith in him was unbounded.

Brack looked quite rakish, so he told himself, when he gazed in a mirror in the hat shop next day, on the way to the station. He had been to the barber's, had his whiskers and mustache trimmed, his hair cut, and a shampoo.

"I'm fresh as paint," he said to Rose, who was glad to see him so respectable. The smell of the sea hung about him, but it was tempered by some very patent hair oil which emitted an overpowering scent.

Several porters spoke to Brack, asking where he was going.

"Doncaster to see the Leger run."

They laughed and one said: "Bet you a bob you don't get farther than Exeter."

"Don't want to rob you, Tommy," was the reply. "I'll give you chaps a tip—have a shilling or two on Tearaway."

"Never heard of him."

"It's a her, not a he."

"Whose is she?"

"Mr. Woodridge's, Picton Woodridge's."

"The gentleman who rode four winners here last Easter, and won the double on The Rascal?"

"The same, and he's given me the tip."

"Nonsense!"

"Gospel," said Brack.

"You must have come into a fortune; it'll cost you a pot of money going to Doncaster."

"Mr. Woodridge is paying my expenses. He kind o' took a likin' to me when he was here; I rowed him to his yacht several times. He's one of the right sort, he is," said Brack.

"You're in luck's way," said the porter he had addressed as Tommy.

"It's men like me deserve to have luck—I'm a hard worker."

"We're all hard workers," said Tom.

"Go on! Call trundling barrers, and handlin' bags hard work? Rowin's hard work. You try it, and you'll find the difference," said Brack.

Tom laughed as he said: "You're a good sort, Brack, and I wish you success. This is your train."

Rose came up.

"I've got the tickets. Is this the London train, porter?"

"Yes, right through to Paddington," said Tom, staring as he saw Rose and Brack get in together.

"Who is he, Brack, your swell friend?" he asked.

"Him? Oh, he's a cousin from Yorkshire," grinned Brack; and Rose sank down on the seat overwhelmed.

CHAPTER XXII

DONCASTER

BRACK and Rose arrived at Doncaster on the eve of the St. Leger, staying at a quiet hotel on the outskirts of the town. The railway journey from Torquay had been a source of anxiety to Rose. Brack made audible observations about the occupants of the carriage, which were resented, and Rose exercised diplomacy to keep the peace. He was horrified to see Brack pull a black bottle out of his bag.

"Beer," said Brack; "will you have some?"

Rose declined in disgust; Brack pulled at it long and lustily, emptied it before reaching Exeter, got out there, went into the refreshment room, had it refilled, and nearly missed his train; Rose pulled, a porter pushed behind, and he stumbled in just in time; the bottle dropped on the floor, rolled under the seat, and Brack created a diversion among the passengers by diving for it. He generously passed it round, but no one partook of his hospitality. It was a relief to Rose when he went to sleep, but he snored so loud he thought it advisable to wake him. Brack resented this, and said he was entitled to snore if he wished.

It was with evident relief that Rose saw him go to bed. When Brack disappeared he related his misfortunes to his host, who sympathized with him to his face and laughed behind his back: he considered Brack the better man of the two.

At breakfast Rose explained what Doncaster was like in Leger week, until Brack, with his mouth crammed with ham, and half a poached egg, spurted out, "You're wastin' yer breath. I've been to see t'Leger many a time."

"Have you? I thought this was your first visit."

"And me a Yorkshireman—go on!" said Brack.

They drove to the course in the landlord's trap, arriving in good time.

"I suppose you have not been in the paddock before?" said Rose patronizingly.

"No; I've been over yonder most times," and he waved toward the crowd on the moor.

"Follow me and I will conduct you."

Brack laughed.

"You're a rum cove, you are. What do you do when you're at home?"

"I am Mr. Woodridge's general manager," said Rose loftily.

"You don't say so! Now I should have thought you'd been the head footman, or something of that kind," said Brack.

"You are no judge of men," said Rose.

"I'd never mistake you for one," growled Brack.

When they were in the paddock Rose was anxious to get rid of him, but he had his orders, and must wait until Mr. Woodridge saw them.

Brack attracted attention; he was a strange bird in the midst of this gayly plumaged crowd, but he was quite at home, unaware he was a subject of observation.

At last Picton Woodridge saw him and came up.

"Well, Brack, I am glad you came," he said as he shook hands. "I hope Rose looked after you."

"He did very well. He's not a jovial mate, a trifle stuck up and so on, gives himself airs; expect he's considered a decent sort in his own circle—in the servants' hall," said Brack.

Picton caught sight of Rose's face and burst out laughing.

"Speaks his mind, eh, Rose?" he said. "You may leave us."

"He's a rum 'un," said Brack. "What is he?"

"My butler; I thought I had better send him for you in case you were undecided whether to come. I am glad you are here; and, Brack, I have a caution to give you. No one knows my brother, he is so changed. If you recognize him, say nothing—it would be dangerous."

"I'll be dumb, never fear," said Brack. "I thank you for giving me this treat; it's a long time since I saw t'Leger run. Your man tells me Tearaway will win."

"I feel certain of it. You had better put a little on her at twenty to one," said Picton.

"I will, and thank you. It was kind to give me ten pounds."

"You deserve it, and you shall have more, Brack. If my filly wins to-day you shall have a hundred pounds and a new boat."

"Good Lord!" exclaimed Brack. "A hundred pounds! It's as much as I've saved all the time I've been in Torquay—and a new boat, it's too much, far too much."

"No, it isn't. Remember what you risked for us."

"That's him, isn't it?" said Brack, pointing to Hector, who had his back to them. "I recognize his build."

"I'm glad no one else has," said Picton. "Yes, that's he."

Hector, turning round, saw Brack, came up, and spoke to him. Picton said: "This is Mr. Rolfe, William Rolfe, you understand?"

Brack nodded as he said: "He's changed. I'd hardly have known his face."

It was before the second race that Hector met Lenise Elroy in the paddock with her friends. She was not present on the first day and, strange to say, he missed her society. It startled him to recognize this. Surely he was not falling into her toils, coming under her spell, for the second time, and after all he had suffered through her! Of course not; it was because of the revenge burning in him that he was disappointed. How beautiful she was, and how gracefully she walked across the paddock; she was perfectly dressed, expensively, but in good taste. She was recognized by many people, some of whom knew her past, and looked askance at her.

Hector went toward her. She saw him and a bright smile of welcome lit up her face.

"I am so glad to see you," she said.

They walked away together, after she had introduced him to one or two of her friends.

Brack saw them and muttered to himself: "That's the lady was making inquiries about him at Torquay, and she doesn't know who he is; she can't. Wonder what her game is, and his? She knows Hackler too. There may be danger. I'd best give him a hint if I get a chance."

"What will win the St. Leger, Mr. Rolfe?" she asked.

"Ripon, I suppose; that is your tip," he said.

"Yes, they are very confident. His owner is one of our party; we are all on it. Have you backed anything?"

"I have a modest investment on Tearaway; I am staying at Haverton with Mr. Woodridge," he said.

"You appear to have faith in the filly."

"Oh, it's only a fancy; she may not be as good as they think," he said.

Picton saw them together. He was surprised, startled; he thought of Hector's remark about keeping his eyes open. He recognized Mrs. Elroy, although he had not seen her for several years. What a terrible risk Hector ran! Was it possible she did not recognize him, that she really thought he was William Rolfe? It seemed incredible after all that had happened. Was she deceiving Hector as he was her? Picton remembered his brother had spoken about a plan, and revenge. What was his intention? If Mrs. Elroy did not know he was Hector Woodridge, then indeed his brother had a weapon in his hands which might help him to awful vengeance; the mere possibility of what might happen made Picton shudder. Hector had suffered terribly, but was it sufficient to condone a

102

revenge, the consequences of which no one could foresee? They appeared quite happy together. Had his brother fallen under her spell for the second time? No, that was not possible; it was not in human nature to forgive such injuries as she had inflicted upon him. Mrs. Elroy saw Picton, recognized him, and said to Hector: "That is your friend Mr. Woodridge, is it not?"

"Yes; do you know him?"

"No."

"Would you care to be introduced?"

"As you please," she replied; she was thankful when Picton went away with Sir Robert, and the introduction was avoided.

"There will be an opportunity later on," said Hector. "When are you returning to town?"

"After the races, on Saturday."

"From Doncaster?"

"Yes."

"What train do you travel by?"

She named a train in the afternoon.

"May I have the pleasure of your company?" he asked.

"I shall be delighted if you wish it."

"I do," he said. "Nothing will give me greater pleasure."

"Then I shall expect you," she said, with a glance he knew well, as she rejoined her friends.

Undoubtedly Lenise Elroy was one of the most attractive women at the races; there was just that touch of uncertainty about her mode of living which caused men to turn and look at her, and women to avoid her when possible.

Sir Robert Raines, when he saw her, said to Picton: "I wonder she dare show her face here in Yorkshire; some women have no shame in them."

"She is a wicked woman, Bob; she ought to be in prison instead of poor Hector. I believed at the trial she shot Elroy, and I always shall," said his wife.

"Who is that beautiful woman who was talking to Mr. Rolfe?" asked Rita.

"She is Mrs. Elroy," said Picton.

Rita knew nothing about Hector's troubles; she was young at the time of the trial.

Something in his manner of speaking caused her to ask: "You do not like her?"

"No; she is a woman with a past, a very bad past, but she faces it out, and is recognized by some people. I should not like you to know her," he said.

"Men are very unmerciful to a woman who errs," she said.

103

"If you knew as much about her as I, you would agree with me that she ought to be treated as an outcast; she is not fit to be in the company of respectable people," he said bitterly.

This was so unlike Picton that she felt he must have strong grounds for what he said. Her curiosity was aroused; Mr. Rolfe might enlighten her.

"Let us go and see Tearaway," she said, and at the mention of his favorite's name Picton's face cleared, the shadows flitted away, he was himself again.

Brant Blackett came up hastily, a troubled look on his face.

"What's the matter?" asked Picton anxiously.

"Erickson's been taken suddenly ill," he said. "I'm afraid he'll not be able to ride."

CHAPTER XXIII

THE CROWD IN THE RING

THIS was a serious matter indeed. Erickson knew the mare well, having ridden her in several gallops; in addition he was a clever, capable rider. It would be a great misfortune if he could not ride.

Picton went with his trainer at once, leaving Rita with her brother and Hector.

Fred Erickson looked pale and ill; he was not a strong man.

"I'm afraid I can't do the filly justice," he said, "but I'll ride if you wish, Mr. Woodridge. I feel a trifle better now, but I'm weak."

"I'd like you to ride, Fred, if you can manage it. I can't get a suitable jockey at the last minute."

"Then I'll do it. Will you get me some brandy?"

The trainer went for it, a small group gathered round, Erickson looked very pale, there were whispers that he would not be able to ride. These quickly spread, and when some of the people from Haverton village heard the rumor they were very much upset; all had pinned their faith to, and put their money on, Tearaway.

Several came to Picton, asking him if there was any truth in it; he said unfortunately there was, but that Erickson would be able to ride, he thought. With this they had to be contented and wait. It was an hour before the St. Leger was to be decided. Fred Erickson pulled himself together, but he was afraid he would not be able to do the mare justice; he would try his best, she was so good that if he managed to stick on and guide her she would run her own race and probably win.

Sir Robert Raines spoke to him; he was very anxious, he had a large sum at stake.

"Feel any better, Fred? I hope so; we are all depending on you to pull through."

"I'll manage it somehow, Sir Robert," said the jockey, "but I'm not myself at all. I wish I were. There'd be no doubt about the result then."

"But you are strong enough to ride, you'll not give in?"

Fred smiled.

"I'm not one to give in. I'll ride the filly and win on her if I can," he said.

105

"That's right," said Sir Robert. "Can I get you anything? Would a glass or two of champagne brace you up?"

"I've had a liqueur brandy," said Fred.

"That will mix with the champagne. Come with me."

Fred drank two glasses and felt better; the color came back into his cheeks, his hands were firmer, the shivering left him; if only it would last until Tearaway had won.

All was bustle and excitement; the horses were being saddled for the great race, fifteen of them, a larger field than usual.

Ripon was a hot favorite, and it was probable he would start at two to one. He had been second to Snowball in the Derby, and ninety-nine out of a hundred people who saw the race vowed he was unlucky to lose, that his jockey rode a bad race on him, and came too late. Snowball broke down and was scratched for the St. Leger, so they could not fight their Epsom battle over again; even had this been the case Ripon would in all probability have been the better favorite. Bronze, Harriet, The Monk, Field Gun, Hot Pot, The Major, and Dark Donald, were all supported; a lot of money was going on Bronze. Tearaway had been backed at a hundred to five; when it was known Fred Erickson was not well her market position was shaken and she went out to thirty-three to one.

Fletcher Denyer was in the ring. Of late there had been some coolness between him and Lenise. He had no desire to lose her; as he saw her slipping away from him he became anxious to possess her altogether. He recognized at last that he was in love, that she was necessary to him, part of his life, that it would be very dull without her. Chance might put something in his way; he was a believer in luck. If only he could discover something about this man Rolfe, who had come between them. No one appeared to know anything about him. He had made inquiries in various quarters; William Rolfe had never been heard of. It seemed strange, a man with money too, and moving in racing circles, where people generally found out all about each other. Lenise Elroy had avoided him in the paddock, he saw it plainly; it angered him, but he had the sense to know he must not interfere but bide his time.

It was in an ill-humor that he went into the ring. He had been given a "great tip" about Bronze, and, as he was in funds for the time being, he determined to speculate above his average. Bronze was in a stable famous for great surprises. He was a horse that had shown good form but in the summer seemed to go all to pieces and was badly beaten at Ascot and Newmarket. There was, however, no doubt that he had been backed to win a huge fortune for the St. Leger. The famous Doncaster race, in this particular year, was the medium of some wild plunging which was reminiscent of twenty or

106

thirty years before. At least six horses were backed to win fortunes. The plunging on Ripon was desperate, and on Bronze the money was poured like water. The Monk was backed to win many thousands, so were Harriet, Field Gun, and Hot Pot; Tearaway would take sixty thousand pounds or more out of the ring, at long odds, if she won. Small wonder the scene in Tattersalls was more animated than usual. The big bookmakers, aware of every move in the market, kept laying the favorite and others. Their wagers were framed on business lines: only one horse could win and they were taking hundreds on half a dozen or more; if an outsider came to the rescue they would land thousands—with one exception—this was Tearaway. There was hardly a well-known man in the ring who had not laid Picton Woodridge's filly almost to the extent of his book, and more money was coming on for her.

Fred Erickson mastered his feeling of faintness in wonderful fashion. His will helped him, he was determined, and as the time drew near for the race the excitement of the event kept him strung up to concert pitch.

Gradually the filly came back to her former position in the market, but twenty to one was freely offered against her: she was an unknown quantity and this did not augur well for her chance.

Hector went into the ring and put several hundreds on Tearaway; he was anxious to have a good win, and Picton was so sanguine of success.

Fletcher Denyer saw him and, following behind, heard him book several big wagers about Tearaway.

"He can't know much about it," he thought, "to back an outsider like that."

At the same time he was uneasy, for he had a lot of money on Bronze, and had put a saver on the favorite. William Rolfe had shown he was not a man to be taken in: Denyer found that out in one or two transactions he had with him.

He spoke to Hector, asking him what he knew about Tearaway.

"Not much," he replied. "I fancy her, that's all; she's a very good looking filly."

"But you must have some line to go upon. Perhaps she has won a good trial?"

"I am not likely to know that," said Hector.

"Be fair with me, Rolfe. Is she worth a tenner or two?"

"Please yourself. I don't see how she can beat the favorite, or Bronze; but she might—there's no telling," and he walked on.

"Hang him, I believe he knows something about her and he

107

won't enlighten me. He can keep it to himself. If she wins I'll pay him out in some way or other," muttered Fletcher.

Brack had never been in Tattersalls before. The noise, the crush, the yelling of odds, the struggle to get money on, amazed him. He wondered if all the people had suddenly gone mad. He had five pounds in his hands, he knew enough about betting to know what to do.

"What are you layin' Tearaway?" he asked a man on the rails.

The bookmaker looked at him and smiled.

"Twenty to one," he said.

"I'll have five pounds on," said Brack.

"A hundred to five Tearaway," said the bookmaker, and his clerk booked it. "What name?" he asked.

"Brack, but you'd better give me a ticket."

"As you please," and he handed him one. There was a lull in the row for a moment and the bookmaker said to him: "You don't often go to the races, eh?"

"No, not often," said Brack.

"A seaman?"

"Yes."

"Where do you hail from? I've a son at sea."

"I'm a boat owner at Torquay; I used to be at Scarborough."

"Yorkshireman?"

"Yes."

"You seem a good sort. Who told you to back Tearaway?"

"Never mind that. I fancy it," said Brack.

"Somebody must have told you," persisted the man.

"Well, if you want to know and it'll do you any good, the owner told me," said Brack.

The bookmaker laughed.

"You're a cute 'un," he said. "The owner, eh? Mr. Woodridge. I suppose you're a friend of his?"

"I am."

"Good, you'll do. I hope I have to pay you the hundred; it will suit my book," laughed the bookmaker.

"Don't believe me, eh?" muttered Brack as he walked away. "You'll maybe have a better opinion of me after Tearaway's won."

108

CHAPTER XXIV

"BY JOVE, SHE'S WONDERFUL"

THE horses were saddled, the jockeys mounting, everything in readiness to go out for the parade.

Picton was talking anxiously to his trainer and Erickson, last instructions were given, Fred was told to make the most of Tearaway in every part of the race, use her staying powers, and in the last furlong her wonderful sprinting qualities to the utmost.

"You feel better now?" asked Picton.

"Yes, much better," said Fred; but he was anything but strong.

A great cheer broke out from the stands and course.

"That's the favorite," said Picton, smiling.

"Tearaway will make a hack of him before the winning post is reached," said Fred.

"You are the last out. Good luck to you, Fred," said Picton as he rode off. "Well, Brant, what do you think of it?"

"What I have always thought, that she will win."

"But about Fred?"

"He'll be all right; he would not have ridden had he not been confident of himself," said the trainer.

It was a beautiful sight, the fifteen horses, parading in the soft September light, the colors of the riders flashing, the thoroughbreds eager for the fray, well knowing what was about to be required of them. There was a dense crowd on the moor, a real Yorkshire crowd, all horse lovers, enthusiasts, judges; on no racecourse in the world is there a more sport-loving crowd than Doncaster on St. Leger day.

The stands were packed, so were the rings; bustle and excitement on all sides; the only clear space was the course, a bright green grass track, winding in and out amidst a black surging mass of people. Brack surveyed the scene with wondering eyes. It was all new to him, although he had been on the moor, and seen the great race before, he had never witnessed it from the stand side; the contrast was remarkable. It was also many years since he had been on a racecourse.

He was not excited, he viewed the scene calmly; it was not in his nature to bubble over with enthusiasm. As the horses galloped past, and went to the post, he was thinking about Lenise Elroy, what she had said to him at Torquay, and how she had spoken to Carl

Hackler. He wondered if danger threatened Hector Woodridge; he must try and have a word or two with him before he left the course.

Mrs. Elroy watched the purple and white sleeves worn by Banks, the rider of Ripon, the favorite. She wanted him to win. She had, at Rupert Hansom's suggestion, put a hundred pounds on him. Rupert Hansom was the owner of Ripon, a rich man, not particularly popular, living apart from his wife, who had obtained a separation from him on account of his conduct with a well-known opera singer. He admired Mrs. Elroy, would have liked to be intimate with her, but she did not care for him in that way, he was merely a casual acquaintance. Her eyes rested on the saffron jacket and red cap of Picton Woodridge.

"What pretty colors!" she exclaimed.

"Mine?" Hansom asked.

"No; they are very nice. I was looking at that peculiar yellow jacket and red cap."

"They're Woodridge's colors—saffron, red cap. I don't think Tearaway has much chance, although I hear they have backed her for a large sum," he said.

So that was Tearaway! What a splendid black mare, and how well the colors of the racing jacket contrasted with her dark shining coat.

There was not much time for reflection; in a few minutes they were sent on their journey, getting off in an almost unbroken line, a splendid start.

Round the bend they swept, a moving mass of brilliant colors. The Major held the lead, stretched out to his full extent, half a dozen lengths in front; he was followed by Dark Donald, Bronze, Harriet, Ripon, The Monk, Field Gun, and Tearaway, the remainder well up.

The Major traveled at a great pace; it was to be a fast run race. He was a very fair horse, although not quite equal to staying the St. Leger course; as a matter of fact, he was out on a pace-making mission for Bronze. At the back of the course The Major still led, the others were creeping up. Harriet was now in second place, Ripon, and Bronze, racing together, Tearaway close behind them, level with The Monk.

The race became more interesting. All the well backed horses shaped well, and their numerous backers watched every move with interest.

Picton worked his way through the crowd and entered his box just before the start. Rita was all excitement; she said Torquay races were very tame after this.

"I don't suppose I shall ever have a chance of riding four winners in two days here, or of winning a double," said Picton.

110

Hector caught sight of Mrs. Elroy's glance and smiled; she was not far away.

Sir Robert was fidgety. He had done what he considered a rather risky thing, backed Tearaway for several hundreds, standing to win a large sum. He considered it risky because he still doubted if the trial on Haverton Moor was quite correct; it seemed too good to be true that Tearaway had beaten Tristram at only seven pounds difference. He had on the spur of the moment said that Picton had the St. Leger in his pocket, but that was merely a figure of speech, the result of over-enthusiasm. He was now watching the race with keen interest, and thought Tearaway too far back.

"Erickson's not making sufficient use of her," he said.

"He'll get through presently," said Picton. "I think The Major made the pace rather hot for the first six furlongs."

"Perhaps that's it," said Sir Robert. "I hope he'll ride it out, I wish that queer sort of faintness had not come over him."

They were entering the straight, when rounding the bend a good deal of bumping took place.

The cause of it was the sudden collapse of The Major, who almost stopped dead, and narrowly escaped knocking Bronze down. Bronze in turn collided with Harriet, and the pair interfered with Ripon, and The Monk, who had come with a fast run, Tearaway was in the center of the course and steered clear of the lot.

Fred Erickson pulled her wide on the outside to avoid any possibility of a collision because he did not feel equal to it. When he saw the interference at the bend he was glad; it was the best thing he could have done.

The consequences of the colliding were not serious; no one was to blame. Fairly in the straight, Harriet took command, followed by Bronze, Ripon, The Monk, and Dark Donald, with Tearaway in the middle of the course.

The race grew more and more exciting. Up to this point the winner could not be picked, half a dozen horses had excellent chances.

"My fellow will win," said Rupert Hansom to Mrs. Elroy.

"I hope so," she answered; but her glance was on the saffron jacket, and the black mare. They looked dangerous.

"He's going well," said Sir Robert.

"Which is going well?" asked his wife.

"The favorite, confound him," he snapped.

Brack had a very good view of the horses as they came up the straight. He saw the bright jacket of Tearaway's jockey in the center of the course and to him it appeared the race was little short of a certainty for her. He was not much of a judge, but he loved racing, and when he saw the black mare, out alone, catching the leaders, he shouted for joy. Some one told him to make less noise; it had no effect on him, he still continued to talk to himself, and give vent to an occasional cheer.

Fred Erickson rode a great race. Tearaway was going splendidly; he felt a glow of pride in her, was glad he had such a mount, for he had not yet won a St. Leger, it had long been his ambition to do so.

Halfway down the straight something seemed to stab him in the chest; his head swam, for a moment he reeled in the saddle, the reins loosened in his hands, Tearaway slackened speed. Half dazed, by sheer force of will he controlled himself. His eyes were dim, he saw the horses in a mist, they hardly appeared real. He took hold of Tearaway and urged her forward, the gallant mare responded, her astonishing speed began to tell.

Blackett saw Fred almost swoon—he had exceptionally powerful glasses—and wondered he did not fall off.

"It's all up," he muttered; then, as he looked again, he saw Tearaway coming along as fast as the wind. The black filly stood out by herself, the saffron jacket alone in the center of the course. On the rails Ripon and Harriet were racing hard, with Bronze drawing up; the trio appeared to have the race among them. Already there were shouts for the favorite, and Rupert Hansom said to Mrs. Elroy: "I told you he would win."

She had seen many races, and did not think Ripon would win. She feared the black filly, who was going so fast, catching the leaders. She wondered Hansom did not see it too.

In Picton's box it was all excitement. Fred Erickson was seen to swerve in the saddle, then recover, and send Tearaway along at a terrific pace.

"Well done, bravely done, Fred!" exclaimed Sir Robert.

"Splendid!" said Rita.

"She'll win!" said Picton as he watched her, the perspiration standing in beads on his forehead.

"I think she's a chance," said Hector; "but Ripon is forging ahead, and Bronze is not done with."

"Look at her now!" said Picton.

"By jove, she's wonderful!" said Sir Robert.

CHAPTER XXV

FAST AS THE WIND

A ST. LEGER long to be remembered. Three horses abreast fighting a terrific battle a furlong from the winning post; in the center of the course a coal black mare, coming with a beautiful even stride, at a pace men marveled at. Old hands who had seen Hannah, Marie Stuart, and Apology win, later Dutch Oven, and La Flèche, Throstle, and the peerless Scepter, were astounded at Tearaway's speed.

On came Picton Woodridge's black filly, the saffron jacket showing boldly, Fred Erickson sitting motionless in the saddle. How still he sat! No one knew he dared not move; had he done so he felt he must fall off. With desperate efforts he retained his seat; he alone knew what a great performance Tearaway was putting in, that she was carrying more than a dead weight, that if anything he hampered instead of assisting her.

Ripon got his head in front of Harriet and Bronze, and the shouting was deafening.

"Ripon wins!" yelled Rupert Hansom.

Mrs. Elroy was looking at Tearaway. The black mare was gaining fast, she would get up and win, she had no doubt about it. She was mortified because William Rolfe had not told her the real strength of the mare and her trial. He ought to have done so; they were friends. What was his reason? Was he jealous of her being with Rupert Hansom? Perhaps he was, and thought she would tell him about the mare. If this were so, she did not mind losing her hundred. He had promised to meet her at the station and journey to town with her; much might happen between Doncaster and London—possibly he might propose. She intended to urge him on in every possible way, and she possessed remarkable powers of fascinating men and was aware of it. These thoughts were mixed up in her mind as she watched the saffron jacket. The great mass of people on the rails, and standing on forms behind, at last saw that Tearaway was dangerous. Ripon held the lead, Bronze next, Harriet and Tearaway level. The noise was terrific, the thousands of people surged to and fro, hundreds of them could just see the red cap bobbing up in the center of the course.

Tearaway settled Harriet's pretensions, and caught Bronze. Fletcher Denyer turned pale with rage; he recognized that Rolfe had not given him the strength of Tearaway. It was a shame, after the excellent mining tips he had given him.

Bronze was beaten. He had lost a large sum, more than he cared to pay; when he had settled on Monday there would be very little ready money left, and he must settle or his reputation, such as it was, would be gone. Rolfe evidently knew all about Tearaway; there was no doubt he backed the mare to win many thousands of pounds. The commission agent he worked for said Tearaway was one of the worst in his book, and the bulk of the money had gone to William Rolfe. Denyer introduced Rolfe to the man, who would not thank him for this client whose first wagers were on a winner at thirty-three to one.

Tearaway passed Bronze and drew level with Ripon. Rupert Hansom was quiet now, watching the struggle on which so much depended. His hopes of winning were of short duration. Tearaway wrested the lead from him, passed him, forged ahead, Erickson sitting perfectly still, and won by a couple of lengths, with the greatest ease. The way the flying filly left the favorite was wonderful. Ripon might have been standing still. Banks, his rider, when he realized the situation was amazed. Ripon was a good horse; what, then, must this filly be?

No matter what wins the St. Leger, there are rousing cheers for the victor. It was so in this case. They were given with more heartiness because she was a Yorkshire-bred mare, owned by a popular Yorkshire squire; there was a real county flavor about it, and the men of the wolds rejoiced exceedingly. Some of them lost money on Ripon, but that was a small matter compared with the defeat of the Newmarket champion by a home-bred 'un; patriotism first is always the case with a Doncaster crowd.

"Picton, my boy, I congratulate you," said Sir Robert, wringing his hand. "By gad, I wish the Admiral could have seen this!"

Hector heard the words and turned round quickly; they cut deep into a not-yet-healed wound.

Picton looked hastily at his brother and guessed what that sudden movement meant.

"Thank you, Sir Robert," he said. "It is a great victory. I also wish my father could have seen it," he added in a low voice.

Rita's congratulations came next.

"I am so glad," she said, "so very glad; you own the best mare in England."

"Go down and lead her in, don't waste time here," said Sir Robert; and Picton went.

Hector followed him, glad to get out of the box. "I wish the Admiral could have seen it." Sir Robert's words rang in his ears.

He caught sight of Mrs. Elroy in a box and vowed he would make her pay to the uttermost for the misery she had caused. There was no mercy in him at that moment; the recalling of his father's death steeled his heart, deadened his conscience, made him cruel, hard, almost murderous. She smiled at him and her glance fanned the flame within him.

"To-morrow we journey to London, to-morrow," he thought.

Picton Woodridge was recognized as he came with his trainer to lead Tearaway in. Cheer after cheer was given as he walked beside her through the living lane.

"How are you, Fred?" he asked.

The jockey did not speak, he gazed straight before him with dull eyes, like a man in a dream.

"Brant, he's very ill," said Picton.

The trainer looked at the jockey and was alarmed at the expression on, and color of, his face. There was no spark of life in it and his complexion was a leaden color.

"Keep up, Fred, keep up! You've done splendidly!" said Brant.

Many people in the crowd noticed the jockey's condition and wondered at it.

"He's ill, poor chap."

"The race has been too much for him."

"I heard he was bad before they went out."

"He's a good plucked 'un anyhow."

Many such remarks were passed as Tearaway went in.

"Get down," said Brant sharply, trying to rouse him.

Fred looked at him but did not seem to understand.

"Get down, unsaddle, and weigh in," said Brant.

"Yes, of course, I forgot," said Fred in a hollow voice.

Two of the stewards were looking on; they had just congratulated Picton on his win.

"Your jockey looks ill," one of them said.

"He is; he was very bad, faint, before the race, but he said he'd pull through, and I could not find a good jockey at the last moment," said Picton.

"You might have ridden her," said the other steward. "You are about the weight, and would not have made any difference to the result."

Picton was flattered; this was high praise indeed; the steward was one of the best judges of racing in the land.

Fred managed to take the saddle off and walked with unsteady steps to the weighing room. He sat in the chair with a bump. The clerk at the scales looked at him.

"You're ill, Fred," he said.

The jockey nodded; he would not have been surprised had they told him he was dying. He got up from the scales, and Banks, the rider of Ripon, dropped his saddle and caught him as he fell forward in a faint.

"All right," was called.

Brant came forward; he and Picton carried him outside. A doctor came, ordered him to be taken to the hospital at once, and thither he was conveyed, Picton accompanying him.

When Fred came to, he said to Picton, with a faint smile: "Don't stay here; I'm all right. I did feel bad; I don't know how I stuck on. She's a wonder; she won the race on her own, and carried a log of wood on her back. I was quite as useless; I could not help her at all."

"You are sure you do not wish me to stay?"

"Quite," said Fred. "I shall probably be on the course to-morrow."

"What's the matter with him, doctor?" asked Picton, when they were in the consulting room.

"He's consumptive, there are all the symptoms, and it is weakness caused through that. He may be able to go out to-morrow as he says; it is wonderful how they rally—a flash in the pan. He can't live long, I'm afraid; in any case he ought to give up riding," said the doctor.

"I don't think he'll mind that so much now he's won the St. Leger," said Picton, smiling. He liked the doctor, fancied he resembled some one he knew. "Will you come to Haverton and have a shot on the moor?" he asked.

"You are very kind, Mr. Woodridge, but perhaps when you hear my name you may be prejudiced against me."

"A name can make no difference," said Picton. "What is it?"

"Bernard Elroy."

Picton started; he was much surprised.

"I am the brother-in-law of Mrs. Elroy. Now do you understand?"

"Yes," said Picton. "It makes no difference; all that is past."

"But not forgotten," said the doctor.

"No, it is not. You cannot expect it."

"Mr. Woodridge, if I could prove your brother's innocence, I would. I'd give a great deal to prove it, do anything that would assist in proving it."

"You believe he is innocent?" asked Picton.

"I do not believe he shot Elroy," said Bernard.

"Then who did shoot him?" asked Picton.

116

"There is only one person can tell us that."

"And it is?"

"Mrs. Elroy," said Bernard.

117

CHAPTER XXVI

THE STRUGGLE FOR THE CUP

TEARAWAY was in the Doncaster Cup on the concluding day of the meeting, but Fred Erickson was not well enough to ride, although on the course.

Picton said nothing to his brother about Dr. Elroy. Hector had rather a serious wordy encounter with Fletcher Denyer, who called him nasty names, and plainly said he had willfully deceived him about Tearaway. Hector spoke his mind freely, saying he had no wish to see him again.

"If you think you've seen the last of me, you're mistaken," said Fletcher. "I owe you a bad turn and I'll repay it, I always do."

Hector laughed as he walked away. He told Lenise Elroy of the encounter.

"You must choose between us," he said. "I have no desire to meet him at your flat."

"You can easily guess which I shall choose," she said.

He questioned her and she replied, "You."

"The climax is drawing near," he thought.

"You'll run Tearaway in the Cup I expect?" asked Sir Robert. His favorite Tristram was in, and he had no desire to see the celebrated Cup horse beaten by the flying filly, as he feared would be the case.

"I think so," said Picton. "You will start Tristram?"

"Yes. I must not own up I am afraid of your mare; but, by jove, I am, my boy," said Sir Robert.

"It will be a great race between them," said Picton.

"A real sporting event," said Sir Robert. "It will cause more excitement than the St. Leger."

When it became known on Thursday night that Tristram and Tearaway would oppose each other in the Doncaster Cup, and that Ripon, Bronze, Fair Dame, and Sir Charles, would run, excitement worked up to fever heat. Nothing else was talked about in the town at night, and in all the papers on Friday morning mention was made of the great struggle that might be expected. The Special Commissioner wrote that it was an open fact that Tristram and Tearaway had been tried on Haverton Moor before the St. Leger and the filly had won at a very slight difference in the weights, and he concluded as follows: "This being the case, the Leger winner should

118

be victorious, as Sir Robert Raines' great horse will have to give a lump of weight away, so I shall go for Tearaway to win."

This appeared to be the general opinion; only many shrewd men thought Tristram would prove more than a match for Tearaway over the Cup distance. Another argument was that the severe race in the St. Leger must have taken it out of the filly, while Tristram was fresh, and very fit; in fact, Sir Robert's horse was stated to be better than he had ever been. Bronze, too, was given a chance, as he was a proved stayer; while Ripon was not considered out of it.

Much to Rupert Hansom's disgust, Banks declined to ride Ripon and accepted the mount on Tearaway. At first this seemed somewhat unfair, but Hansom had severely taken the jockey to task over his riding in the St. Leger, and Banks resented it, knowing he had done his best.

"Tearaway is the best filly we've seen for years," he said, "and Ripon had no chance with her; you'll see how it is if she runs in the Cup."

"Perhaps you'd like to ride her?" sneered Rupert.

"I should. I will if I get the chance."

His chance came sooner than he expected. Seeing Picton Woodridge on Thursday, before the last race, the jockey said, "Will Fred be well enough to ride your mare in the Cup, sir?"

"No, he's not at all well, Dick. He's consumptive, I'm sorry to say."

"Have you a jockey?"

"Not at present."

"Will you give me the mount?"

"Are you not engaged to ride Ripon?" asked Picton, surprised.

"No, there is no engagement, and I have fallen out with Mr. Hansom about the riding of his horse in the St. Leger," said Banks.

"You are free to ride my mare?" asked Picton.

"Yes."

"Then you shall have the mount. I would sooner see you on her than any one, except Fred," said Picton.

"Thank you, sir," said Banks, jubilant, and went off to tell Rupert Hansom, who said it was an infernal shame, and raved about it to his friends, calling Banks all sorts of names.

"I don't see what you have to complain of," said Mrs. Elroy. "You said he rode a bad race in the St. Leger, jeeringly asked him if he'd like the mount on Tearaway in the Cup, when he replied he would. It appears he took you at your word and accepted the mount when it was offered him; I think he's on the winner."

"Do you indeed?" he said crossly. "I hope if you back her you'll lose your money."

"How very disagreeable you are," she said. "Men with diminutive minds always appear to lose control over their tempers, and forget their manners."

Rupert Hansom found another jockey in Crosby, a very fair rider.

There were seven runners for the Cup, fields had been stronger than usual at the meeting.

Rita looked supremely happy. She knew what was coming; Picton had more than hinted at it. Before she left Haverton he would ask her to be his wife; she knew what her answer would be. She loved him, had done so from the first time they met, and she was quite sure he loved her.

Dick Langford also guessed what was about to happen; it pleased him to contemplate Picton as a brother-in-law.

"I'll give him The Rascal as a wedding present," he said to himself, laughing.

Before they went to the races on Friday he said to Rita: "Picton's having a great week—the Leger, the Cup to-day, a wife before the week's out."

She laughed as she replied: "That's a treble—better than his double on The Rascal."

"You're worth the winning, Rita," he said kindly. "Wonder what I shall do without you."

"Find a wife," she said.

"Expect it will be compulsory; it is not good for a man to live alone," he answered.

A tremendous crowd witnessed the Doncaster Cup. It was as memorable a race as the St. Leger; many thought it more so.

Sir Robert secured the services of May, a reliable jockey, at times brilliant.

"I hope I shall beat you," he said to Picton.

"I hope Tearaway will win," was the laughing reply.

"It will be a great race," said Dick; "but my bit goes on the mare."

"And mine," said Rita.

"And mine," said Hector.

"All against me," laughed Sir Robert. "My hundred or two goes on Tristram."

"Robert, I don't think you ought to bet. Remember the trial," said his wife.

"You against me!" he exclaimed. "I am in a terrible plight indeed."

The horses were out, seven in number, a real good lot.

Sir Robert's face glowed with pride as he heard the roar of

120

cheers which greeted the red jacket and black cap, and his good horse Tristram. Another roar was given for Tearaway; the others were all cheered lustily. They were soon on their journey, Sir Charles making the running, followed by Fair Dame, Bronze, and Harriet, with Ripon, and Tearaway next, and Tristram last. Sir Robert's horse never went to the front in the earlier stages of a race.

Rupert Hansom gave Crosby instructions to keep in touch with Tristram and Tearaway.

"You've nothing else to fear," he said; "and remember there's a hundred for you if you win."

Sir Charles soon dropped out of it and Harriet took his place. At the back of the close the lot closed up, half a dozen lengths separated first and last.

In the straight they swept; then a change took place. Ripon made the first move forward, followed by Tearaway and Tristram.

Up the straight they came at a terrific pace, for Tearaway had gone to the front, and Banks was making every use of her great speed and staying powers.

Cheer after cheer pealed over the course when the saffron jacket was seen in the lead; the filly was favorite, a six to four chance.

Banks kept pushing her along; he did not know how to handle her as well as Fred Erickson, but did his best.

May was riding Tristram strictly to orders.

"Bring him with a rush in the last quarter of a mile," said Sir Robert.

Ripon was going well, but could not keep the pace with Tearaway.

At last May brought Tristram out and the great horse came along with giant strides, his natural style of going. On he came swooping down, passing first one then another, drawing level with Ripon, leaving him, and going in pursuit of Tearaway.

The excitement was intense; all eyes were fixed on the splendid pair, the mare and the horse, owned by two good sportsmen, hailing from Yorkshire, both well known in the county. Captain Ben Bruce was with Brack, who had been persuaded to stop until the meeting was over; he was very fond of the old boatman, and knew he deserved well of them all. Brack was to have a look round Haverton before he returned home. He had backed Tearaway again, and was shouting her name frantically, much to the Captain's amusement. She looked like a winner, she was going so well, but there was no mistaking the way in which Tristram galloped.

"He's catching her!" said Sir Robert excitedly.

Picton smiled confidently; he did not think he would do it.

121

A great shout went up when Tristram got to Tearaway's girth; May rode a brilliant finish.

Banks handled the filly well, but had not the same powers as Fred Erickson at his best; they were wanted now just to help her home.

Neck and neck they raced, head and head, not an inch between them, outstretched nostrils; it was a tremendous race, one of the best ever seen for the Cup.

Sir Robert and Picton looked on, thrilling with excitement. It was a desperate finish. Both were game, the filly and the horse, and fought to the bitter end. As they passed the judge's box no one could tell which had won.

"Dead heat," said the judge.

Sir Robert and Picton shook hands heartily.

"By jove, what a race!" the baronet said.

"I'm glad it was a dead heat," said Picton. "We've both won."

CHAPTER XXVII

THE RESERVED COMPARTMENT

LENISE ELROY arrived at the station and looked around for Mr. Rolfe. He was not there; at least she did not see him. As the time drew near for the departure of the train she became anxious; she hoped much from this railway journey in a reserved compartment: they would be able to talk without interruption.

Hector had seen Brack, who explained how Mrs. Elroy had questioned him at Torquay, and also Carl Hackler.

"You'd best be careful," said Brack; "I saw you talking with her on the course."

"She has no idea who I am. I thank you all the same," he answered.

"Mr. Woodridge has given me a hundred pounds and a new boat," said Brack.

"And you richly deserve it! Here's a twenty-pound note to add to it," said Hector.

"I'll be a rich man before I get back to Torquay," said Brack.

"Here you are; I thought you were not coming," said Mrs. Elroy, as Hector came up.

"There's plenty of time," he said; "ten minutes."

"You can't think how anxious I felt."

"Why? You could have gone on alone."

"That would not have suited me; I want your company," she said.

They were shown to a reserved compartment, the guard locking the door until the train started; it was crowded, and some of the race-goers are not particular where they get in.

"It's a non-stop train; we are alone until we arrive at King's Cross," said Hector.

Lenise was at her best. She confessed she was really in love this time; she meant to find out how matters stood with him.

Despite all she had done, he felt her charm still. She was not a good woman, far from it, but there was something so subtle and attractive about her he found it hard to resist the spell.

The thought of Sir Robert's words, "I wish the Admiral could have seen this," gave him courage. It had to be done—why not do it now? There was no escape for her; it was not a corridor train; they were boxed up for three hours or more. She looked at him with

123

softly gleaming eyes; her whole being thrilled toward him; she had never been so fascinating.

"You are quiet. What are you thinking about?" she said. "Reckoning up your winnings on Tearaway, I suppose."

"My thoughts were far away from there," he said.

"Where were they wandering?"

"I was thinking about you," he said.

"How nice of you," she said quietly.

"You prefer me to Fletcher Denyer?"

"How can you ask such an absurd question?"

"I was wondering whether I loved you; I was thinking whether you would be my wife, if I had the courage to ask you."

"Try," she said, her eyes on him.

"Do you really love me?" he asked.

"You know I do; you must have known it from the first time we met."

"There should be no secrets between us," he said. "I have something to tell you."

She turned pale, a faint shiver passed through her; he noticed it. Would she confess what she had done?

"I too have a confession to make, if you love me, and wish me to be your wife."

"Otherwise?"

"I shall keep my counsel; it would not interest you."

"Let me tell you something first," he said.

"As you please, confidence for confidence," she said with a faint smile.

"I have not always lived a decent life," he said. "I once committed a crime, I paid the penalty, I was sent to prison, to Dartmoor."

She started again, a look of fear was in her eyes.

"When I told you I was mining on Dartmoor it was not true; I worked on Dartmoor, but it was as a prisoner. I was in the same gang as Mr. Woodridge's brother."

"You were," she said in a hollow voice, wondering why he told her this.

"Yes, poor fellow. I never saw a man so broken down in my life; his face haunted me. I said something about it before, you may remember."

"Yes, I recollect," she said.

"We had very little chance of speaking but I heard his story in fragments, how he hated the woman who had brought him down so low. He swore to me he did not kill the woman's husband, but he

124

would not tell me who did, although I asked him many times. From what I heard I came to the conclusion she fired the shot."

His eyes were on her; she could not face their searching glance.

She made no remark, and he went on: "It was mainly through me he escaped," he said. "When I was released I searched out his brother and made a suggestion. Mr. Woodridge has no idea I was in prison; he thought I had been abroad for several years. Needless to say, I did not enlighten him; I will trust you not to do so."

"I shall never speak of it."

"Does this alter your opinion of me? Shall I go on?" he asked.

"I love you," she said. "I shall always love you, no matter what happens."

"As you know, Hector Woodridge escaped."

"But he is dead."

"That is uncertain. He may be, or he may have got away and be in hiding. He must be greatly changed, no one would recognize him," he said.

"It is hardly possible," she said.

"Perhaps not, but still he may be alive, and if he is, the woman who ruined him had better beware. I believe he would kill her if he met her. What have you to confess to me? You see I have placed my character in your hands; you can ruin me socially if you wish."

"I do not wish, and I thank you for the trust you have placed in me," she said. "I am afraid to confess all to you, afraid you will never speak to me again when you know who I am."

"Who you are?" he exclaimed.

"I told you, when you remarked on the curious coincidence that my name was Mrs. Elroy, that I was not the Mrs. Elroy connected with Hector Woodridge's case."

"Well," he said.

"I told you a lie. I am the same Mrs. Elroy. It was my husband Hector Woodridge shot. It was me he was in love with."

He looked at her without speaking for several minutes. The silence was painful; he was thinking how to launch his thunderbolt, how best to trap and overwhelm her. There was no escape, she was entirely at his mercy.

"You ruined Hector Woodridge, sent him to penal servitude for life," he said.

"I was not entirely to blame. We loved, or at least we thought so."

"How did it happen?" he asked.

"The shooting?"

"Yes."

125

"It was quite unpremeditated; had the revolver not been there it would never have happened. I believe my husband intended to shoot him, and me—it was his revolver."

Hector wondered if this were true.

"The revolver was on a small table. I saw it but did not remove it; had I done so the tragedy would not have happened."

"Why did you leave it there?" he asked.

"I do not know; probably because I did not wish my husband to know I was afraid. I was aware he had found us out, that an exposure must come sooner or later. He was madly in love with me; I almost hated him, he was so weak, almost childish, and I wanted a strong man to rule me. Shall I go on, do you despise me, look upon me as a very wicked woman?" she asked in a strained voice.

"Go on," he said; "tell me the whole story, how he was shot, everything."

"I will, I will make a full confession; but be merciful in your judgment, remember I am doing this because I love you, that I do not want it to stand between us, I plead to you not to throw all the blame on me. Hector Woodridge was a strong man and I loved him, I believe he loved me, he overcame all my scruples. I yielded to him, gave myself to him—surely that was a great sacrifice, my name, honor, everything for his sake. We were together in my husband's study. We thought he was in London, but he did not go; he set a trap and caught us. I shall never forget the look on his face when he came into the room. I saw his eyes rest on the revolver, and I felt it was our lives or his, but we stood between him and the weapon.

"Hector Woodridge guessed what was in his mind; he must have done so, for he laid his hand on the revolver. My husband saw the movement and said, 'Put that down, you scoundrel,' and advanced toward us. Hector raised the revolver and told him to stand back. He did so; he was afraid.

"There was an angry altercation. I remember saying I was tired of him, that I would live with him no longer, that I loved Hector Woodridge. This drove him to distraction; he became furious, dangerous; he would have killed us without hesitation had he possessed the revolver, there was such a murderous look in his eyes. Does my sordid story interest you?" she asked.

"It does; everything you do or say interests me," he said.

"And you do not utterly despise me, think me too bad to be in decent society, to be sitting here alone with you?"

"Go on," he said in a tone that was half a command, and which caused her to feel afraid of something unknown.

"At last Elroy's rage got the better of his prudence; he made a dash forward to seize the revolver, raised in Hector's hand. It was

126

the work of a second, his finger was on the trigger; he pulled it, there was a report, Elroy staggered forward, fell on his face, dead," she said with a blanched face, and trembling voice.

"You pulled the trigger," he said, calmly looking straight at her.

127

CHAPTER XXVIII

HOW HECTOR HAD HIS REVENGE

THIS direct charge so astonished her that for a few moments she did not recognize its full significance. She sat wildly staring at him, completely overwhelmed.

He watched; her terror fascinated him, he could not take his eyes off her.

She tried to speak and failed, seemed on the point of fainting. He let down the window; the cool air revived her, but she was in a deplorably nervous condition.

At last the words came.

"I pulled the trigger?" she said. "What do you mean, how can you possibly know what happened?"

"I said you pulled the trigger. It is true, is it not?"

"No; Hector Woodridge shot my husband," she said in a low voice. She was afraid of him; his knowledge seemed uncanny—or was it merely guesswork?

"That is a lie," he said.

"How dare you say that!" she said, her courage momentarily flashing out.

He smiled.

"I thought this was to be a full confession," he said.

"I will say no more; you do not believe me," she said.

"Then I will continue it," he said, and she seemed petrified with fright. He gave her no chance. He related the history of the trial; so minute were his particulars that she wondered if he were a man, or a being possessed of unearthly knowledge.

"Hector Woodridge was condemned to be hanged, and you spoke no word to save him. Your evidence damned him, almost hanged him, sent him to a living tomb."

"I could not lie; I had sworn to speak the truth," she faltered.

"You did not speak the truth," he almost shouted; and she shrank back, cowering on her seat. She wondered if he had suddenly gone mad. Impossible. His knowledge was uncanny.

"Had you spoken the truth you would have saved him; but you dared not. Had you told all he would have been set free, you would have been sentenced. You were too much of a coward to speak, fearing the consequences; but he, what did he do? He remained silent, when he might have saved himself and proved you guilty."

"It is not true," she murmured faintly.

"It is true," he said fiercely. "Think what he has suffered, think and tremble when you imagine his revenue. I will tell you something more. You were in Torquay when he escaped. You were at supper one night; there was a chink in the blind; footsore, hunted, his hands torn by the hound, his body all bruised and battered, hungry, thirsty, every man's hand against him. Hector Woodridge looked through it, he saw you feasting with your friends."

"Stop!" she cried in an agonized voice. "Stop! I can bear no more. I saw his face, I have never had a peaceful moment since."

"I shall not stop," he said harshly. "Outside he cursed you, prayed for justice, and another chance in life."

"How do you know all this?" she asked in a voice trembling with dread.

"Never mind how I know; sufficient that I know," he said. "Hector Woodridge, thanks to an old boatman, escaped and boarded the Sea-mew, his brother's yacht, lying in Torbay."

Her agitation was painful, her face became drawn and haggard, she looked an old woman. Rising from her seat, she placed her hands on his shoulders, looking long and searchingly into his face.

"Sit down," he said sternly, and she obeyed.

"He was taken away on the Sea-mew. He went mad, was insane for some time, then he fell dangerously ill; when he recovered he was so changed that even the servants at Haverton, who had known him all his life, failed to recognize him."

"He went to Haverton?" she said.

"Yes; he is alive and well. No one recognizes him as Hector Woodridge; he has assumed another name and once more taken a place in the world. To all who knew him he is dead, with two or three exceptions. The prison authorities think he is dead; they have given up the search for him. He is safe, able to carry out his scheme of revenge against the woman who so cruelly wronged him. You are that woman, Lenise Elroy."

"And what does he purpose doing with me?" she asked faintly. "You cannot know that."

"I do; I am his most intimate friend."

She started; a weird, unearthly look came into her face.

"His one object in life is to prove his innocence. He cannot do that unless you confess," he said.

"Confess!" she laughed mockingly. "There is nothing to confess."

"You know better, and you will be forced to confess or else—"

"What?"

"If you do not prove his innocence he will—"

"Kill me?"

"That may happen, under certain circumstances, but he wishes to give you a chance."

"He has asked you to speak to me?"

"Yes; he was at Doncaster."

"At the races?"

"He saw you there. Something of the old fascination you exercise over him came back, and for a moment he wavered in his desire for revenge."

He saw a faint smile steal over her face.

"He told you this?"

"Yes, and more; but I have said enough."

"You have indeed. You have brought a terrible indictment against me, Mr. Rolfe; if it were true I ought to die of shame and remorse, but it is not true, not all of it," she said.

"Lenise, look at me. Do you love me after all I have said?"

"I do. Nothing you can say or do will ever alter that."

"And you will marry me?" he asked. "It is a strange wooing."

"I will be your wife. You will save me from him; you will try and persuade him I am not deserving of a terrible revenge," she said.

"Are you afraid of him—of—Hector Woodridge?"

She shuddered.

"Yes," she said, "I am."

"Supposing he were here, in this carriage in my place?"

"I should fling myself out," she said. "I should be afraid of him; it would be terrible, awful. I could not bear it."

"Because you know you have wronged him. Do the right thing, Lenise. Confess, prove his innocence, think how he has suffered for your sake, how he has kept silent all these years," he said.

"Why do you torture me? If he has suffered, so have I. Do you think the knowledge of his awful position has not made me shudder every time I thought of it? I have pictured him there and wished I could obtain his release."

"You can prove his innocence," he said.

"Supposing I could, what then? What would happen? I should have to take his place."

"And you dare not."

"I am a woman."

"Then you will not help to prove his innocence?"

"I cannot."

Hector got up quickly, took her by the wrists and dragged her up.

130

"Look at me, Lenise. Look well. Do you not know me?"

He felt her trembling; she marked every feature of his face. Gradually it all came back to her, overwhelmed her. She traced feature by feature—the eyes were his eyes, yes, the face was his face. He saw the dawn of recognition come over her and break into full light. She knew him; her eyes dilated with terror, her cheeks went ashen pale, her lips were colorless, her limbs trembled, she could hardly stand.

"Yes," he said. "It is I, Lenise, Hector Woodridge, and you are alone with me in this carriage."

"Mercy, Hector, mercy, I am only a woman."

"And you love me, you said so, you love William Rolfe?"

She sank on her knees, she clasped his limbs, looking piteously into his face. He saw how she suffered.

"Get up," he said; "do not kneel there."

She hid her face between her arms, he heard her sobs, saw they shook her frame. The train rattled on, whirling at a great pace, drawing nearer and nearer to London. She moaned, it cut him to the heart to hear her. A fierce struggle went on within him, a battle with his strong will. He placed in the front rank the memory of all he had suffered, then brought up his father's death, the cruel disgrace, as a reserve to support it. He had his enemy beaten at his feet, he was victor, it was a humiliating defeat for her.

"The quality of mercy is not strained."

Strange how the line should come into his mind at this moment. He had always been a student of Shakespeare, he knew much of it by heart, in prison he repeated whole parts, and it solaced him.

"Lenise, get up."

His tone had changed, she raised her tear-stained face. What she saw in his look made her cry out:

"Hector, is it possible? Speak to me, Hector! I know you now. Oh, what a fool I have been! I have always loved you, but I was a coward. It was you, not William Rolfe, I loved again when we met. You were Hector Woodridge and my soul went out to you. Do with me as you will. I am strong now, for I believe you love me. I will confess, make it public, tell everything. You know I did it. The revolver was in your hand, your finger on the trigger, I pulled your hand and it went off. I will make it known if only you will forgive me. God, what a fiend I have been to let you suffer so! And you have kept silence all these years for my sake!"

She spoke rapidly; he knew she was in earnest and his heart softened. He had loved her deeply, he loved her now, he had always loved her, even in his bitterest moments in prison, when he had

131

framed a terrible revenge. It had been his intention to marry her in his assumed name, and on their wedding night tell her he was Hector Woodridge and then—well he shuddered at the mere thought of how near a brute he had been.

Hector was never more of a man than at this moment. He had won a great victory over himself, far greater than over the woman at his feet. He had conquered revenge, utterly crushed it, cast it out forever.

He stooped down and raised her gently.

The train hissed on, carrying its living freight, drawing nearer to London.

She hung her head; he raised it, looked straight into her eyes, then kissed her.

From that moment Lenise Elroy was another woman. She felt the change instantaneously; she was transformed, she knew whatever happened she would be true to him, that she would love him with a devotion that could not be surpassed.

He kissed her again as he held her in his arms.

"This is my revenge, Lenise," he said.

CHAPTER XXIX

AN ASTONISHING COMMUNICATION

AT Haverton everything shaped well. Picton asked Rita to be his wife and she consented. They were very happy, Dick rejoiced exceedingly, Captain Ben was pleased, Brack congratulated them in his quaint way before he returned to Torquay.

"I'll give you The Rascal for a wedding present," said Dick. "I hope he'll win the National for you."

"He will have a good chance," said Picton. "It is a very welcome gift."

"I think you and Rita will be happy," Dick said.

"We shall, and when she is mistress here there will be a delightful change for the better," said Picton.

"I hope there will be no collision between Rita and Mrs. Yeoman," laughed Dick.

"No fear of that. She is very fond of Rita; she told me so, said she was very pleased I was going to marry her."

"Then that's all right," said Dick.

He and his sister remained a week longer, then returned to Torwood; Rita and Picton were to be married from there early in the New Year.

Dr. Elroy came from Doncaster for a few days' shooting. Picton liked him, so did Captain Ben. The doctor was an excellent shot, and accounted for many brace of grouse; he also showed some knowledge of horses, which at once ensured Brant's good opinion.

It was during the doctor's stay Picton received a letter from his brother, containing an enclosure. Both astonished him immensely, and small wonder.

He read them carefully twice, and decided that Hector's wishes should be obeyed. These were to the effect that Picton should read them to Captain Ben, Sir Robert Raines, and any other persons he thought desirable should know the truth. Picton decided Dr. Elroy should join them when he read the letter. Sir Robert received a hasty summons to Haverton.

"Wonder what's in the wind now," he said.

"A trial I expect," said his wife.

"You and Mr. Woodridge think of nothing but horses."

"I have had a communication I wish you to hear," said Picton. "I have heard from my brother."

"Hector!" exclaimed Sir Robert.

"Yes. He is alive and well. He knows you are to be trusted; he wished you to hear all he has written. You will be surprised to learn William Rolfe is Hector."

"Good heavens!" exclaimed Sir Robert. "Do you know, Picton, my boy, I thought he resembled him, but of course I had no idea he was Hector. It's wonderful; how did he get away?"

Picton gave him an account of Hector's escape and how he boarded the Sea-mew, and all that followed.

"The strangest part of the story is better told in his own words," said Picton. "I wish you, Captain Ben, and Dr. Elroy to hear it."

Sir Robert was lost in wonder at such strange happenings. When they were all seated in Picton's study he asked them to promise to keep everything secret, which they readily did, when he explained whom the communication was from.

Picton began Hector's letter, which, after a few preliminaries, read as follows: "You know how I escaped, and thanks to the good farmer on the moor, and with the aid of Brack, boarded the Sea-mew and got safely away. Then, taking the name of William Rolfe, I came to Haverton and no one knew me. I wish it to be thought that Hector Woodridge is dead, that I am William Rolfe, and shall always remain so, for reasons which I will explain, and which will cause you great astonishment. Something wonderful has happened since I left Haverton, something that surprises me even now, and which I can hardly understand, yet it is an accomplished fact, and I shall never regret it.

"I met Lenise Elroy at Doncaster station by appointment; we traveled alone in a reserved compartment. You have some idea of the vengeance I intended taking upon her, but you have no conception how terrible it was to be. I purposed carrying it out in the train, declaring to her who I was—she thought I was William Rolfe. I gradually led the conversation up to a point when I could relate to her how Hector Woodridge escaped and boarded the Sea-mew, and that he was alive and well, living under an assumed name. I posed as his best friend. She was amazed, and frightened, at the minute details I gave her, thought it uncanny. There was a dramatic moment when she explained what happened when Elroy was shot, in order to clear herself, offer an excuse for her conduct. She said Hector Woodridge pointed the revolver at Elroy and as he advanced, fired. Then I said, 'You pulled the trigger.' This, as you may imagine, was a knock-down blow for her; she almost fainted. She denied it, of course; it was a critical moment. Then I bade her look in my face, asked her if she recognized me. Gradually she did

134

so; she fell on her knees, clasped my legs, sobbed as though her heart would break. She confessed all. She said I held the revolver pointed at Elroy, but she pulled my hand back, and it went off, killing him. I enclose a confession she has signed to this effect. It proves my innocence. I did not actually fire the shot, although I leveled the revolver at him, to frighten and keep him back. I had no intention of shooting him; as God is my judge, I did not wish to take his life. She acted on a sudden impulse; perhaps she wished to pull my hand down, thinking I intended shooting him, and, as my finger was on the trigger, it went off. It was all a terrible blunder, which she and I have suffered terribly for. You little know how she has suffered; she has told me and I believe her. What I suffered no one can imagine, but I believe I can learn to forget it under the new conditions of life I have mapped out.

"As she knelt at my feet sobbing, a strange revulsion of feeling swept over me. Before all this happened she acknowledged she loved me as William Rolfe, that she had done so from the first time we met.

"I looked down at her and spoke gently. She noticed the changed tone in my voice and raised her head. 'Hector!' she cried in strange surprise.

"Stooping down I raised her gently. I felt no desire for revenge; all my savage feelings were swept away. I loved her, loved Lenise Elroy, who had so deeply wronged me, with an undying love. I knew I had always loved her, even when in prison, and my feelings were bitterest against her. She saw something of this in my face. I kissed her and held her close to me. From that moment, Picton, I forgave all, she was very dear to me. No matter how she had sinned I knew she had always been mine. I remembered how she surrendered herself to me; I recognized that I had tempted her, as she had tempted me; that we were both guilty, that had I behaved as a man, and kept away from her, the tragedy which blighted so many lives would not have happened.

"We sat side by side and did not speak. The wonder of it all swept over us and held us silent. We looked into each other's eyes and read our thoughts. She was transfigured, a different woman, a new soul had entered her body, she was not the Lenise Elroy of old days. I felt all this; I was certain I could rely upon her. She spoke at last, and said she would write a confession which I could place in your hands to do as you wished with; she would abide the consequences. I have sent this to you, Picton, knowing you will never make it public, but hide it in some place until our deaths take place. You can read it to our old friend Sir Robert, and Captain Ben,

135

and any one else you think ought to know, and that you can depend upon to keep silent. It is short, but true, and she has signed it.

"Perhaps the strangest news of all for you is that we are married, and are now Mr. and Mrs. Rolfe. I wished it to take place at once, and she was willing to do anything I asked.

"As Mr. and Mrs. William Rolfe, we sail for Melbourne in a fortnight, where I shall go up country and buy a small station somewhere. We intend to keep out of the world, to live for ourselves. Lenise wishes it, she says a lifelong devotion to me will only help to blot out the past. Of her love I am certain; she is not demonstrative, but I catch her sometimes unawares, and her face expresses her thoughts. Forgive her as I have, Picton, write her a kindly letter, tell her she has done right, wish her happiness in her new life. We shall not come to Haverton; it is better not.

"I won a large sum over Tearaway; I had a thousand pounds on her at a hundred to three. I do not want any more money. Keep the dear old place up; some day we may see it, but not for years—it may be never. I should like to see you, Sir Robert, and Captain Ben, if you will meet me in town, just to say farewell. I hope you will be happy with Rita; I am sure you will. At some future time you may tell her the tramp she treated so kindly on his way to Torquay was your brother Hector. I have Dick's coat she gave me; I shall always keep it as a treasured remembrance of a good woman's kindness and sympathy. Remember always that Hector Woodridge is dead, that William Rolfe lives, and is a settler in Australia. In that great country we shall be surrounded by new scenes, faces, and places; no one will know us; we shall live our lives peacefully until the end.

"The storm is over, Picton, and calm come at last. This is how I took my revenge. How strange are the workings of Providence, how sure is His eternal justice, how wonderful and mysterious His ordering of all things!"

Picton then read Lenise's confession, which exonerated Hector from blame. It was brief and to the point; she did not spare herself.

"I'll tell you what, Picton, Hector's a great man, an extraordinary man, he deserves the highest praise we can give him," said Sir Robert, and with this they all agreed.

"Remember, Hector is dead, William Rolfe lives," said Picton, and again they agreed to abide by this decision.

CHAPTER XXX

TEARAWAY'S PROGENY

IT was a quiet wedding and Dick gave his sister away. A few friends met at Torwood to bid them speed on their honeymoon, which was spent at Florence. On their return they went direct to Haverton, and Mrs. Woodridge settled down to her duties as mistress of the house, with Mrs. Yeoman as her trusty guide.

Rita was supremely happy; Picton told her Hector's story when they were in Florence.

"So I was right when I thought I recognized Mr. Rolfe as the man who asked me for help, or rather whom I assisted on his tramp to Torquay," she said.

"Yes, you were right," said Picton. "You made a greater hit than you were aware of."

Picton schooled The Rascal over stiff fences on Haverton Moor. A four-mile course had been specially mapped out by Brant during his absence in Italy, and the fences were as high as those on the National course.

"You'll find 'em formidable," said the trainer, "but if he's to jump the National course so much the better."

Picton soon found, as he had thought when he won on him at Torquay, that The Rascal was a great fencer. The ease with which he went over the biggest jump without a mistake proved this, and Brant grew enthusiastic about his chance. Rita was nervous when she saw Picton riding over these great jumps, but The Rascal seemed to fly them so easily she gained confidence and eventually became as keen about his winning the National as Picton himself.

Everything went well with his preparation; the horse was as sound as a bell, and under Brant's tuition became quiet and docile.

The Rascal liked Picton, he and his rider were on excellent terms, they knew exactly how they felt toward each other. A week before the Aintree meeting Dick Langford came to Haverton. He was surprised when he saw the improvement in The Rascal, grew enthusiastic as he watched Picton ride him over the big fences.

"I'd no idea he could jump like that!" exclaimed Dick.

"I had when I won on him at Torquay," said Picton.

"Do you think he's a chance in the National?" Dick said to the trainer.

"He has, Mr. Langford, a ripping chance. I can't pick out

anything to beat him, and he's got such a nice weight, only ten stone; he'll gallop them all to a standstill. And as for fencing, he'll fly Beecher's Brook like a bird."

Neither Rita nor Picton, nor their many friends who saw the race, will ever forget that memorable Grand National. What an awful day it was! The March wind howled and whistled over the course, biting and stinging, cutting the face almost like a lash. Then sleet fell, followed by a whirling snowstorm, which had not abated when the horses went out. The course was heavy, dangerously slippery, but for all that not bad going. It was all against the top weights.

The Rascal lashed out as he felt the stinging half-frozen particles whipping his skin. He put back his ears, lowered his head, and took a lot of persuading before he faced the blast. Most of the horses protested in the same way.

Then the sun gleamed out, the snow ceased, and for a few minutes it was bright and clear.

They were off, twenty of them, and a glorious sight it was. Rita stood with Captain Ben, Sir Robert, and Dick. They had an excellent view of the course; had it been clearer they would have seen the whole race.

When the horses had gone a little over a mile, snow fell again, the sun disappeared in the gloom, the light became bad.

Picton could hardly see the jumps, so blinding was the storm; but The Rascal saw them and despite slipping, and an occasional stumble, cleared them. Once he rapped hard; this roused him and for the remainder of the journey he did not make a mistake.

It was an extraordinary race. Horse after horse came down, until at the last two jumps only three were left in. Another fell, then Mortimer came down at the last obstacle, and The Rascal came in alone, being the only one to finish the course. It was a day of triumph for Picton and his friends. A big stake was landed, a big double, the St. Leger and the Grand National won for the famous saffron colors.

The Rascal and Tearaway were the pets of the Haverton stable. The former won at Manchester and Sandown, Picton riding him. The filly won the Great Metropolitan and the Ascot Gold Cup, following this up with a veritable triumph in the Cesarewitch, carrying nine stone. She then retired to the stud, and was mated with her old opponent Tristram, to the huge delight of Sir Robert, who prophesied the result would be a remarkable equine prodigy. The Rascal ran in the National again and fell, the only time he came down in a long and wonderful career; Picton had a nasty spill and was brought back in the ambulance. This was a shock to Rita; she longed for the time when he would give up steeplechase riding, but she never hinted at it, she knew how passionately fond of it he was. The Rascal won the great 'Chase again the following year, thus setting the seal on his fame by carrying top weight to victory.

By this time Picton and Rita had two sons; this was followed in due course by two girls; so they were supremely happy and all went swimmingly at Haverton. They had troops of friends. Picton became Master of the Haverton Hounds, and his popularity was unbounded. Rita was regarded as a ministering angel when she went abroad, scattering good things around in the depth of winter, and all the poor blessed her name.

Brack retired from active service, but had half a dozen boats and was a popular favorite at Torquay. Picton never forgot him at Christmas, or the farmer on the moor, who had helped Hector to escape.

Carl Hackler often chaffed Brack about the escaped prisoner and said he was not quite sure yet whether he had not smuggled him on board the Sea-mew.

Brack, however, was as close as an oyster, and Carl got no satisfaction in this direction.

Far away across the ocean, in Australia, about fifty miles from Ballarat in Victoria, Hector and his wife settled down, as Mr. and Mrs. Rolfe, on a small station with a picturesque homestead and excellent paddocks surrounding. They were happy, but there was one shadow hanging over their lives which had not yet lifted. They could not forget; it was impossible. They never alluded to it, but they knew it was there. Still, they were contented and made friends in the new land. They were prosperous. Hector took kindly to the life. He worked; his hands all liked him. He had a fine herd of cattle, a hundred good horses, sheep on a large run he had just taken over, in addition to Willaura, his homestead.

Lenise had her share in the stock: she owned a few horses, a couple of Alderney cows, and a large number of poultry of various breeds with which she took prizes, and of which she was very proud. After ten years came the crowning of her life. She had a son, and in bearing him she almost lost her life. Never till he felt her slipping away from him had Hector known how much he loved her. When she recovered, after a long illness, she said to him:

"I feel we are forgiven. Our child has lifted the shadow from our lives. We must think of the past no more; we must live for him and the future."

Picton received frequent letters from his brother, and answered them. In one he wrote to Hector that it was evident he never intended returning to England, and that the only chance of seeing him again was to go out to Australia. "Rita says she would like the trip, and it would do us both good. Captain Ben is a trustworthy friend to leave in charge of Haverton, so don't be surprised if some day we arrive at Willaura."

"Do you think she would like me?" Lenise asked her husband.

"Yes; no one could help liking you," he replied.

"Do you ever regret marrying me?" she asked.

"That is a foolish question. You know I do not. Never ask me again," he said.

Hector sometimes went to Melbourne. On one of his visits he saw a broken-down man in Bourke Street and recognized him as Fletcher Denyer. He gave him a wide berth and did not mention it to his wife. He heard once or twice from Brack, who in one letter said: "Brother Bill is a free man again—I reckon you know what that means; the man who did it confessed on his death-bed. He looks after my boats. He's a good sort, is Bill. Mr. Picton never forgets me. He's a good sort too. So are you; so's everybody to me."

"Tearaway's stock are doing wonders," wrote Picton. "Her best are by Tristram, and Runaway is a champion. I think he will turn out the best she has had, and he is by Sir Robert's old favorite, and will probably be the last he will get, as he is very weak and ailing but hobbles about in his paddock. I am sending you out as a present a six-year-old horse by Tristram-Tearaway. He should make a splendid stallion. You can expect him landed in Melbourne in about eight weeks from now. We tried Runaway this morning and Brant says he is like his mother—as 'fast as the wind.'"

THE END